The
Rocky
Orchard

The
Rocky
Orchard

Barbara Monier

. . . .
. . . .

Hide and Seek
Cover art by Sandra Dawson
sandradawson.net

First Edition   ISBN 13: 978-1-937484-82-8

AMIKA PRESS

466 Central AVE #23 Northfield IL 60093   847 920 8084
info@amikapress.com   Available for purchase on amikapress.com

Edited by John Manos & Ann Wambach. Designed & typeset by Sarah Koz. Set in Old Claude, designed by Paul Shaw in 2004, and Minion Pro, designed by Robert Slimbach in 1990. Thanks to Nathan Matteson.

Barbara Monier loves to hear from readers.

Sign up for her mailing list to receive news
about her latest projects: barbaramonierauthor.com.

You can email her directly at bmonierauthor@yahoo.com.

● ● ●

"The distinction between the past, present and future
is only a stubbornly persistent illusion."
                                        —Albert Einstein

Fore word

Fore
word

●●●

I am barefoot. My absolute favorite thing. I reach
down with one toe, just my big toe, to give us the
barest little push to keep the swing going. I feel tiny
grains of dirt on the porch floor as my toe kisses against them.
The extra length of the swing's chain clanks against the chain
that supports the swing, hanging taut from the porch ceiling.
How long has this swing been here? We have never once had
to fix it or adjust it or anything. Not like the old wooden swing
outside, with its long ropes hanging from a high, sturdy branch
of the giant pine. We have had to fix that swing a million times.
My father would drag out the extension ladder and raise it to
very near its full, tottery height to replace the swing's cord.

Despite the density and girth of the rope's tight braids, over time the cables would begin to gray, then blacken as mold crept its way through the thickness. At some point the mold turned to rot. The rot ate its way through, one strand at a time. We knew to sit cautiously, gingerly, onto the seat of the swing, lest it be the moment when the last thread of the rotten rope broke and we were destined to end up plunged into the bed of pine needles blanketing the ground. Then, my father on the ladder, again. But the porch swing has never broken. I toss my head back and look up at the ceiling bolts that hold the swing in place, ancient and painted over so many times, the barest hints of pale orange rust beginning to leak through the pigment. The thought of the bolts' strength, their endurance, amazes me. And makes me tired, exhausted. The strain of years upon years of holding up the weight of human beings. I twirl the extra chain through my fingers; I clunk it against the taut chain that is doing the work of holding us up. I look over at you. My Eddie.

A line of sweat is just beginning to break out in the crease of your neck. I want to capture the expression on your face and put it in a jar. I want to carry the jar around with me like precious fireflies from a summer night. I have never seen you so relaxed, so contented. As if you know what I'm thinking, you reach for my hand and you kiss it. I am staring at you and you know that I am staring at you, and I tear up and you laugh. You kiss my hand again. You have that shy-but-formidable look, the one you had on our first date, our real first date. The look that makes your one dimple sing out. The look that made me think that maybe, just maybe, we might end up right here someday, swinging on this swing.

The summer that I was twelve years old, my girlfriend Karen and I spent the whole afternoon at a swimming pool I'd never been to before. We sat in the sun and talked about boys and laughed and swam and splashed each other and waited for our favorite songs to get played over and over on the transistor radio we'd brought with us. By the end of that afternoon, I felt a kind of deep peacefulness I'd never known before.

Karen's mother had rented a convertible for a special date with Karen's dad, and she came to pick us up from the pool in that convertible. It was the first time I'd ever been in one. The three of us crowded together in the front seat. Karen's mom had gotten her hair done in a fancy French twist for the date, and she tied a chiffon scarf around it for the ride home. Karen turned on the radio, and her mother cranked it up even louder. My body had that cool feeling that stays deep inside of you when you've been in the water all day, but your skin heats up from the warmth of the sun and you feel the hot and the cool all at once. When we hit the road, the wind tossed Karen's and my long, soaking wet hair all over the place, occasionally smacking ourselves and one another in the face. All of those feelings together, it was thrilling, electrifying, but the peacefulness was still there, too. That's what it was like meeting you, Eddie. Just exactly like that.

Your hand in mine is sweaty. The cool moistness of your palm against mine sends a ripple through my body, a shudder of feeling. I reach across your body to trace the line of sweat on your neck with the index finger of my other hand. I taste it. The salt of you. I cannot get enough of you.

You lean your head toward mine. You are going to kiss me. How many times have you kissed me, and my stomach still does a little leap? Your head jerks. What was that? you say. What was what, I ask. I didn't hear anything. I definitely heard something, you say. You didn't hear that? Sounds like someone is throwing something—balls or something like that—one after another. Listen, you say. I hear it. Sounds like it's getting closer, you say. Sounds like it's coming from the orchard. You hear it, right? you ask me. Yes, I hear it.

Stay here. I'll check it out, you say. Probably some kid having a little fun, you say.

Don't be silly. I'll come, too, I say.

The short step down from the porch, my bare foot on the hot summer grass, I am hit by a wall of humidity. The full, fertile feel of the air that marks a Pennsylvania mountain summer. Thick, wet, ripe with a steaming, green life. "I love you as certain dark things are to be loved, in secret, between the shadow and the soul." That poem, the Pablo Neruda poem that you recited. The humidity reminds me. Down on one knee in an old-fashioned gesture I never would have guessed. Holding my hand and you said, "I love you as the plant that never blooms but carries in itself the light of hidden flowers."

The wall of humidity pushes against me. Your arm reaches out and you tell me to stay back. Please, you say. Please stay back. "Thanks to your love a certain solid fragrance, risen from the earth, lives darkly in my body."

4

I see him, you say.

Then I see him, too.

I wonder what in the world he is doing here.

Without thinking I start to call out to him. I want to laugh. I want to wave and ask him what in the world he is doing here.

Then I see his face. "Lives darkly in his body."

And I know what he is doing here. I know.

Part I

Twelve
years earlier.

I . . .

It all began with that party. Well, that's when it started to go south, anyway, in a long, slow, painful, unraveling train wreck. It was the first party like that one that I'd ever been to. I didn't even know the girl—the one whose parents were away that night—but I sure knew that Samantha had legendary status as COOL. I just thought of it as a chance to be out with my new boyfriend—my very first one—without any grown-ups around. And at night!—which was rare, because I was only thirteen years old. Mostly Sean and I hung out at my house or sometimes at my friend Doug's house after school. But then he asked me if I wanted to go steady, and he gave me this enormous ring. It had a smooth black surface with the profile of a knight or some similarly medieval-looking face carved on it. The ring was gigantic on me. I wrapped tons of bright gold yarn all around the back so it would fit me. That ring got me through the long fall days of my freshman year. I looked at it, fiddled with it. I ran my thumb back and forth across the coil of yarn over and over, then worried that the beautiful gold would get dingy and ugly from my constant rubbing. I made sure to walk through the halls between classes carrying my books so that the ring stuck out there in clear, overgrown view.

I was on a cloud at that party. Sean and I held hands and wandered from one dark, candlelit room to the next in this little house with no adults. I was awed and scared and trying really hard to not be quite so awed or scared, and I thought to myself: *So, this is what people do, when they can do anything they want.*

I wasn't sure if Samantha had removed furniture to make room for the party or if her family didn't have much furniture in the first place. Even though the house and its rooms were small, the sparseness gave the impression of their being cavernous—a chair here, a sofa there—with vast amounts of space in between. What sparse furniture there was looked like the things my grandmother and her sister had in their side-by-side duplexes—that old, stiff velour-type fabric that looks like it's going to be buttery soft but actually has little fibers that poke and dig into your skin and chafe you. It didn't look like a real home but more like an abandoned house where someone had haphazardly stuck random things here and there. I thought it was magically exotic.

When Sean introduced me to Chad Howe—who was an absolute *legend*—I thought I might faint. Chad's grandfather had founded a military academy, and Chad had parlayed that heritage, together with his flowing hair, skinny-boy looks, Buddy Holly horn-rims, and shockingly deep, authoritative voice into a high school persona that shot him into the stratosphere of Hip Kids Who Mattered. Chad was so charismatic, he seemed like someone who was destined to have his own cult following. It felt like Chad looked straight into my soul when he said a quick hello before helping his girlfriend—who had a plaster cast from her toes to her mid-thigh and went by the name of Tonya—into the back of a friend's van. Tonya wore a fluttery, fraying dress that must have been dazzling when someone had worn it to cocktail parties thirty years earlier. With the coolness of the evening, she had donned Chad's overly large army jacket. Between the faded glory of the dress, the military jacket, and the enormous cast, I was thoroughly enchanted. I didn't just admire Tonya…I wanted to be Tonya. Chad ceremoniously closed the van door, giving a quick nod to a number of hangers-on who had surrounded him. They stood around for a while, staring at each other and kicking at the ground, and eventually shuffled away.

Oh my god, I thought, *he's having* sex *in that* van! *I am thirteen years old, and I am at a party where Chad Howe is having* sex *with his girlfriend in a van! How totally cool is that?!*

Sean wrapped his arm around my shoulder and whispered

in my ear, "I'll be right back. Gonna go talk to a friend."

"Of course," I said. "Oh, I'll go with you. Want me to?"

"Nah, something I got to talk to him about. Be right back."

The time that Sean was gone—it could have been a minute, it could have been an hour—blurred into a series of images and impressions. Samantha sitting in an old armchair by herself in a dark corner. Her head hanging down so low that her long, deep brunette waves fell completely across her face. Nodding ever so slightly in time to the music. I wondered if Samantha was okay, thought maybe I should go up to her and ask her, but then got worried that maybe that was a weird thing to do. Maybe I would be bothering her, interrupting something I didn't even understand. Plumes of incense and cigarette smoke twirled madly whenever someone moved. A guy wore round, blue sunglasses in a night-black house. Songs began and ended abruptly with the awful noise of a needle scratching across vinyl whenever someone decided to change the music.

When Sean wandered back beside me, he was different. Woozy seeming. He chuckled a little to himself and mumbled something I couldn't understand.

"Sorry, what?" I asked him.

"What the hell were you doing talking to that guy?"

"What guy?" I said. I looked around the room as well as I could in the incense and smoke-laden darkness, but couldn't figure out for the life of me who he was talking about.

"Don't fuck with me. You were definitely talking to him." Sean had never sworn at me before, not once. I was taken aback, but pretty quickly ashamed of myself for not being cooler with it. Sean held up his hand, with his palm really close to my face. I couldn't tell what in the world I was supposed to be looking at. Then I saw it. A circle. A perfect circle, faintly reddish-brown, traced the periphery of his entire palm. "It's from a candle. I put my hand right on the candle and held it there."

"What?" I said, grabbing his hand to look at it more closely.

"I did it to prove my love for you," Sean said.

"You did *what?*" I choked.

Just then, this guy standing at the front door yelled out, "Hey, is there somebody here named Mazie?" For a second, I didn't even move. And the guy added: "Hey, Mazie, if you're out there somewhere, your dad's here. To take you home, I guess."

"Yeah, yeah, I'm Mazie," I said and sort of raised my hand like I was expecting the teacher to call on me. I made a straight line for the front door, left Sean standing there, didn't even say goodbye to Sam, who was still sitting in the same chair, nearly touching the bottom of her hair to her eyeballs as she examined her split ends at exceptionally close range. I walked out that front door in a stupor of confusion. Sean's voice behind me called out, "Hey, Mazie, you forgot your jacket." He handed it to me and then raised his hand to my father, "Have a good evening, Dr. Mills." Jesus, he sounded so normal! So utterly and completely *normal,* not even a hint of the woozy guy who had just shoved his burned hand into my face.

One look at my father, and I knew he was pissed. Really pissed. He had that look of tightly, but precariously, controlled rage, like any little thing could cause him to fly apart into a million, billion pieces and rain down razor spikes on anyone nearby.

I debated whether it would be better for me to talk first or to wait it out. There was no right answer to that.

The second my car door closed he said, "You're grounded. For a month."

"What!?" I said. I had never been grounded before. Not once. "Why? What did I do?"

"We had no idea where you were. No idea! You never asked us if you could go out tonight. You're home for a month. Period."

"That's not true!" I said.

Sheesh. This whole evening was bizarre beyond belief to begin with, but now this. I knew that I'd asked my parents if I could go to this party—well over a week in advance—and I also knew that they had said yes! This was a really tricky one to know how to navigate. Did they actually forget that I'd asked? Well, they drink a lot. A real lot. So that was always a good possibility. But it wasn't like I could point that out, that maybe they "forgot." No question that would make my situation *worse*. I was pissed! I ASKED them. But showing that I was pissed was also going to make my situation worse. I took a deep breath, I gathered all of the calm I could muster, and I said in a really nice, sweet gentle voice, "Dad, I'm really sorry that we seem to have gotten our signals crossed here. I'm sorry if you and Mom were worried, but…think for a minute. I asked you about this party at the dinner table last week. It must have been last Thursday, because we'd just been talking about my math test.

14

Remember? I told you about the math test and then right after that I asked you about the party—because Sean had helped me study for that test and it reminded me to ask you."

My father remained icily silent.

"Did you and Mom think that I just…disappeared tonight? I would never do that! Come on. I would *never do that!* Sean's friend picked me up, just like I'd told you he would."

I halfway expected the steering wheel to shatter, my father had such a death grip on it. We were most of the way home before my father spoke.

"Did you really ask us? Are you telling the truth? Because if you're lying now, I can't even imagine…," he said.

"Not lying. I swear. At the dinner table. Right after I was talking about the math test."

"You didn't say goodbye when you left tonight," he said.

"It's possible," I said and, I couldn't help myself, I let out an audible sigh. I had to move on quickly for fear that I'd showed frustration in a way that would ratchet my father's rage right back up again. "It's possible that I may not have said good-bye when I left. I'm really sorry if that worried you guys." I let a moment go by and then added, "Am I grounded for a month for that?"

"Let me speak with your mother," he said. "I make no prom-ises until then. Not to mention how hard it was to even find out where you *were* tonight. Jesus Christ."

"Yeah, I don't actually know Samantha very well. That's her real name, but everyone calls her Sam. Different schools. I know a lot of people who know her, though, like Sean and a lot of his friends. I think they all go to the same church or something."

Ok, that was a big fat lie, and I knew it, but I thought the circumstances justified my throwing it in there, seeing as how I had been falsely accused. I was not a liar, generally speaking. That's a bad way to live. I mean, I was a teenager, and I had parents…so, of course I lied. But I didn't usually go out of my way to make up stuff and toss it out there. This was different.

Bullet dodged. I did not get grounded.

Pretty soon after that, I turned fourteen. Sean bought me a giant, apple-scented pillar candle for my birthday. I couldn't believe it. A candle.

... 2

After that party, Sean and I saw each other almost every day after school. We'd usually go to Doug's house—Sean, me, my brother Woo, and Doug. The three of them were best friends in high school and were all two years older than me. We'd listen to records or play cards and eat some snacks. Doug's mom would come home from work, pull up a chair to wherever we were sitting, and light a cigarette. She would ask us about our day. She had a deep, booming voice and smoked like a chimney. Her dark-red lipstick —the only makeup she wore—would stain the filters, deeper and deeper crimson, as she puffed on the cigarette and blew the smoke out with great force, aiming it far above our heads. I didn't know many mothers who worked, and I always thought she looked both professional and exotic in her tailored dresses and sensible pumps.

When it was time to go home for dinner, my brother took the shortcut through neighbors' backyards; Sean and I took the long way around, following the street, so we had that few minutes of the daily walk to be alone. He held my hand the whole way.

One day when we were walking home, he grabbed a handful of fresh snow from the road and put it down the back of my coat. The cold stabbed into my back like a hundred frozen knives. I was stunned! "I can't believe you just did that!" I said to him, and then I did something dorky like stomp my foot or put my hands on my hips. He laughed. And, like it was the funniest thing in the world, he knocked my feet out from under me. I toppled to the ground. I lay there in the street, arms and legs all over the place, totally shocked. "What the hell is wrong with you?" I yelled. "What was that?" I picked myself up and dusted the snow off my whole body and checked to see if I'd ripped the knee of my pants in the place where a big giant ache was starting. He was still laughing. "What the hell is wrong with *me?!*" Sean said. "What the hell is wrong with *you?* Seriously! We're having fun here!"

I felt like the whole world lost any sense of meaning right then, like I couldn't figure out a single thing. I thought it was a mean, awful thing to do to me. But he really seemed to think that it was fun and funny. He was my brother Woo's best friend, and Doug's too. In fact, they both kind of idolized Sean. And

I knew I was a scaredy-cat, weird kid. *Ok,* I thought, *maybe it's me. Maybe this is the way fun looks between a girl and a boy.*

On one of those walks, Sean told me that he wanted to marry me. I was wearing my furry white earmuffs, so I wasn't sure I'd heard him right. He went on, telling me he had a whole plan for our future. He would get through college as quickly as he could—three years with Advanced Placement credits—and get his certification to be a high school math teacher. The two of us would get married and move to Hawaii. He had less than two years left of high school, so he figured all of this could happen in less than five years. He'd be about twenty-one. I'd be nineteen. It was not the cold of the late fall evening: I felt that thing that happens to me sometimes. It's like all the blood rushes into my cheeks and my ears. It feels as if flames are going to shoot out from the tops of my ears, and my cheeks are going to explode from the pressure.

Sean started talking about our future a lot, Hawaii this and math teacher that. He also said that I didn't have to worry, that he had "total respect" for me, so he'd never, ever try to push any sexual agenda on me. We would wait until we were married.

This was heady stuff for a young girl such as myself, especially it being my very first time out in the world of dating and boys and relationships. I felt so many different, mixed-up things. Part of me felt valued and cherished and loved. Part of me also felt seriously gypped. Sort of like: Hold it! Isn't it kind of the idea of being a teenager to do some experimenting and try some things out? Maybe even do some seriously stupid stuff and chalk up at least a couple of life lessons and heartfelt regrets and things that will one day be eye-rolling memories? I hadn't even had time to *find out* about stupid stuff I might want to do! Plus, seriously, he wasn't going to even reach a *hand* up to one of my *boobs* over the *next five years?* Is that even *normal?* Not to mention that he had prefabricated my entire life—without talking to me about it!—even though he steadfastly maintained that once he was teaching in Hawaii, he would support me spreading my proverbial wings in whatever ways I could possibly want, forever and ever.

I felt like something was seriously wrong with me. Sean was one of the cutest guys I had ever known. With his jet-black wavy hair, pale skin, ruddy cheeks, and piercing blue eyes, Sean looked like he should be on posters advertising travel to Ireland. He was also one of the smartest guys I knew. And funny. Quick funny. With a lopsided smile he whipped out to enhance his sarcasm. The smile alone made my hands turn clammy and my stomach lurch. And, he had chosen me.

Clearly anyone would think this was the dream boyfriend of all time. Why didn't I feel that way?

I figured the best thing to do was to just pretend. Pretend long enough that I'd start to feel what I was supposed to feel.

...3

The first time I saw *How the Grinch Stole Christmas* was 1969, the same year that Sean was my boyfriend. We watched it together, Sean and I and Doug. My brother wasn't there somehow, even though we were at my house.

We watched *Grinch* in a lightless room, something my family never did. I had been told that watching a bright screen with no other light in the room was reckless and hazardous and could have tragic consequences, which remained vague and therefore almost mystical. Doug sat at one far end of the sofa, Sean at the other. I curled up with my feet resting against

Doug and my head in Sean's lap. Every so often, he reached down and touched my hair.

The magnificently long-suffering but loyal and philosophical dog Max. The clenched-hearted Grinch. The village of Whos whose joy at their mutual sense of belonging transcends all evils. Snuggled between two Nice Boys, I felt safe and warm and protected and loved in a way that was precious and rare.

When the boys left, my parents said They Had to Talk with Me. I was certain that I was going to get clobbered for watching the television set in the dangerously dark room. A terrible wave of guilt shot through me, a pang at having been so lulled, so incautious.

My parents stood shoulder-to-shoulder in a rare moment of solid alliance. My mother said, "Never, ever put your head in a boy's lap."

This was so entirely unexpected, it took me a minute to even decipher the words. The meaning. And when I did, I was even more bewildered. "What?" I said.

My father bid a hasty retreat to the kitchen.

"Your head was in Sean's lap. That's not something you can do. Ever."

"What?" I said again, scanning her face for some clue as to what in the world she meant.

"It's not fair. To the boy," my mother said. "It's too stimulating."

My mother bit her lip.

…4

By this time the holiday season was in full swing. And even though I wasn't exactly religious anymore and thought it was kind of sugary and sentimental, I had to admit that the idea of going Christmas caroling with my old church youth group put a giant grin on my face.

It was far colder than usual for mid-December, and a snowstorm that had been predicted for later that night had begun hours before expected. Houses were decorated, lights twinkled everywhere, it was blustery and freezing and snowing furiously hard—to my mind, a picture-perfect backdrop. The combination of cold and the fact that I didn't sing very often made me light-headed and giddy.

Other than the hot chocolate being completely disgusting, lukewarm, brown water and—as always—a couple of the Usual Kids had poured a flask of vodka into their cocoa and were using an inordinate amount of effort to remain sort-of upright, I was having a pretty great time. Singing. Christmas! A boyfriend!! Sean and I had been going together for nearly three months.

And then everything took a dark, dark turn.

"Don't fuck with me." It was the second time he'd sworn at me. But this time, there was an edge in Sean's voice I had never heard before.

"Of course, I was talking to him. I've known him since I was, like, six years old." The party. Déjà vu. All over again. Sean thinking I was talking to another guy.

"What were you saying to him?" Sean asked.

"What was I saying?"

"Yeah."

"What was I saying? I don't remember! I've been talking to everyone!" Probably my voice exposed a bit of frustration by that point, but I was really trying to be nice. And calm.

And despite what I knew to be true, I was overtaken with the sense that I had done something very, very wrong. I figured I must have. This was my boyfriend—my raven-wavy-haired, intensely blue-eyed boyfriend—and he was clearly MAD. Surely it must be me.

"Sean, I'm sorry. I can't even remember what we were talking about. It wasn't important."

"Well, you sure looked fucking happy."

"What?"

All of the other kids had trickled back into the church, leaving the two of us alone in the driving snow.

I realized that I didn't have boots on, just regular shoes. My feet were rapidly getting soaked. "Shit, my feet are freezing," I said. "Can we go in?"

"You don't give a shit about me." That's what Sean said.

"What? That's not true! Sean, you know that's not true." I felt confused and guilty about having done something I didn't even understand and frustrated with both of us and angry with myself that I could not figure out how to fix this. My toes felt like they might burst through my shoes with the sting of the cold. "Come on, let's go inside. I'm really freezing." And I threw in one final, "I'm sorry. I really, really am." I treated this the same way I treated the whole marriage thing—like this was something I didn't understand one bit, so I better pretend that I did and act normal and assume that it was all my fault.

He reached one hand into an inside coat pocket and pulled out something that I strained to see. The moon—or maybe it was one of the streetlights that flooded the church parking lot and lit up the whirling snowflakes—glinted off the object in Sean's right hand. It was a razor blade. A gleaming, silver straight razor.

Before I could even react, before I had time to consider being afraid, Sean had spun on his heels and was loping through the shin-deep snow, the long fringe of his buckskin jacket flying everywhere. A final flash of metal and moon. His arm fully outstretched. The silhouette of his back quickly vanishing against the mad snowflakes and the black winter sky. I knew that this would be an image I would remember my entire life. The raised arm, the winter moon, the frantic snowflakes, and, most of all, the fringe of his buckskin jacket flying helter-skelter.

I ran after him, ten or twelve steps perhaps, before my feet were thoroughly soaked and freezing. I knew I'd never be able to catch him, and no sign of him remained. Still, I stood there. Alone in a church parking lot. Gathering the courage to walk back inside and figure out all the things to say, to do, after that.

When my ride dropped me off back at home, I crept in the back door and gripped the edges of the stainless-steel sink in the kitchen, not sure if I might vomit. But when my mother poked her head around the kitchen doorway and asked me how the caroling had been, I said, "Fine. Fun."

That was as much of an answer as my parents would expect from their fourteen-year-old daughter. My father had overheard the exchange from the dining room, and my parents both beamed widely as I brushed past them. They didn't notice that I was clutching my stomach with white-knuckled fingers as I climbed the stairs to bed.

Sean showed up the next day after school like nothing out of the ordinary had happened. My ears got that on-fire feeling. He seemed both amused and irritated when I tried to hint around about where he'd gone and what had happened after I saw him at the church. Finally, he shrugged and said something about being in a bad mood and not wanting to have to face his parents. He had gone from car to car in his neighborhood until he found one with an unlocked door. And he spent the night in the car.

It had been freezing cold. Freezing. "Jesus," I said, "are you kidding me?" And I got all worried and protective. He acted like my being worried was quaint and adorable, but that I was hopelessly naive and sheltered. He said he did it all the time. He said his parents didn't even mind; they knew he'd be back. He was the oldest of six kids in a loud, chaotic Irish family, and sometimes, he said, it was best not to be there.

Then I got all worried about his family and what might be going on there. His sister Sheila was in the same grade as me at school and was the living definition of the words meek and mousy. Still, she seemed cheerful enough. She'd been in the same class as me a bunch of times and seemed right straight out of the normal book, so far as I could tell.

I got up the courage to ask my brother Woo what he thought about Sean, *really* thought about him. Like was he playing with a full deck? My brother treated me just like Sean had—like it was maybe a tiny bit cute that I was asking and worried, but he was mostly annoyed and even sort of embarrassed that his baby sister couldn't understand how entirely cool Sean was and how basically inexplicable it was that Sean seemed to be so dead set decided on *me* in the first place.

One Saturday morning Sean came over to our house. Woo

and Sean and I were sitting on the couch together, waiting for Doug to show up so we could all go to the mall to walk around and then ice skate. I sat in the middle—as always—with the boys at either end. Sean lifted his arm to put it around me, and his sleeve pulled back just enough for me to see that his wrist was wrapped around and around with gauze bandage. And when I looked, I saw that the other wrist was, too.

I had no idea what to do.

I sat bolt upright on the couch and whipped around to look at Sean. Of course, he figured out why. He winked at me and tousled my hair. My stomach lurched, and I thought I was going to throw up. I swallowed hard and my mouth fell open a little. Sean gave me a fake punch on my arm, like why couldn't I just be a good sport and stop overreacting to every single thing that happened all the time.

I didn't know if he was right. I felt like I didn't know one single thing. I felt sad and sick and like I needed to vomit or faint or jump up and run away and keep on running. I couldn't deal with it. I wanted out. Of the whole thing. I felt like I was the world's worst human being, ever, in the history of the world, for being scared of a guy everyone else thought was a total champ.

But I didn't care. I needed to get out of this as soon as I could.

...5

Sick. I felt sick, fucking sick, when the telephone rang. I wanted to snatch the old twenty-pound, rotary dial monstrosity of a phone right out of the wall and fling it through the window. I wanted glass to shatter and fly in a million directions and create rainbows of light in midair. I wanted the shards to rain down razors and cut the room into little ribbons. *I'm too young for this,* I thought. *I'm fourteen years old, and I am too young for this. For this shit, for this utter shit.*

"Hello," I said into the receiver.

"I'm pointing a knife at my stomach," Sean said. "Tell me why you broke up with me."

Suicide was just a word, a vague concept. Something whispered, read about in books. Nothing that had ever come near my own world, just a specter keeping itself hidden and far away. I had not even read *The Bell Jar*, hadn't thought of Sylvia Plath turning on the stove in the apartment where she lived every day. Had not been stuck with the picture of her putting her head into the oven with the gas jet running, her two young children sleeping in their beds on the other side of the wall.

Daddy Mommy, I thought. *I don't know what Sean is going to do. I'm scared. I think he's going to do something to himself. Help me, Daddy Mommy. I need your help*, I thought.

But I didn't say anything. Not to my parents, not to anyone.

Sean's younger sister Sheila, the one who was in my grade, the one whom I knew, was the first one home that night. She found him. Still alive, but unconscious.

It's a blur after that. I can picture flashing lights and sirens and a lot of people and a lot of running around, but that doesn't really make sense. They wouldn't have been at my house; all of that would have been at Sean's house. Still, I have a sense of a million faces looking at me. I felt as if the whole world was staring at me. Some with concern. Some people blamed me; I could see it in their faces. Most people were torn, anguished even, between the part of them that wanted to stare at me and the part of them that wanted to look away. I'd become scary to people somehow. So many different things that people felt when they looked at me.

All I'd done was broken up with a boy. A crazy boy.

All I wanted to do was get to the farm. After it all happened. I needed to be there.

...6

I stole my parents' car. Well, would you call it stealing, really? I "borrowed" it without their permission, without them knowing. And, it was two years before I had my actual driver's license, but that's kind of a technicality. My parents had been letting me drive since the summer. Every time we went up there, to the farm, they would take me out driving. Everybody does that in the country. Yes, city streets and the high speed of the expressway were a little unfamiliar, but I figured it out well enough. I just had to be there.

Everybody thinks of the woods as being so quiet, but they're not. Most of the year, they're noisy. Really noisy. Birds and frogs and toads and crickets and cicadas and branches snapping and leaves blowing. But it's a good noise, the kind of noise that lets you think. The kind that opens up your brain instead of suffocating it. But it was winter when it all happened with Sean. A fresh snowfall of nearly a foot blanketed the countryside around the farm; the woods had a completely different sound. It was a kind of silence, but thick, somehow. The sounds were muffled, but you could sense that they were there, behind a curtain. It was ominous and dazzling, all at once.

I parked the car behind the house like my family always did. When I got out, I just started running, right for the creek. The water moved fast enough that it rarely froze completely in the winter. I could hear it after I had run just a few feet. I stumbled in the snow in my headlong, blind rush to get there. I could tell from the tumult that the creek was high, that the water would be roaring over the rocks. While I was still a distance away, I reached down and took off one boot and then the other and pitched them into the snow. I did the same with my socks. And I ran straight into that creek, the water so high that it reached my mid-calves and drenched my pants. Fiery, sharp stabs shot all the way from the bottoms of my feet straight into my brain, and I just stood there. I stood there with my feet in the creek until I was sure that in one more second my legs would buckle underneath me; they would no longer be able to hold my weight. In one more second, I would not be able to get out of the creek, would not be able to run back to the house. I sobbed from the pain, my breath coming in great frozen gasps.

I made a dive for the bank of the creek and lay face down in the snow, my frozen legs and feet waving in the air toward the winter sky.

...7

My mother was the one who came to get me. With my brother Woo.

My father insisted that there be no telephone at the farm—no intrusive contact with the outside world. No way to call and see if I was there. They probably had a pretty good idea about where I had gone, but there was no way to be sure unless somebody ventured there to look for themselves. I thought about how pissed and discombobulated they probably were to have been stranded with one car for three drivers in a suburb where you could walk pretty much all day and not get anywhere at all.

So, it wasn't unexpected when I heard the first distant rumble of an approaching car. I was sitting on the porch, rocking on the swing despite the unforgiving temperature of the January day. My mother was driving my father's van, as I had taken her car. Woo was in the passenger seat. I hated driving that big old van in the winter; its steering and brakes were so hit-and-miss on ice and snow that I called it the Flexible Flyer. My mother hated it, too.

She stayed on the road, didn't pull into the far driveway and across the wide lawn to park by the house like we always did. She'd never done that before. She stopped the van right on the road. I could see her and Woo from where I sat on the swing. Woo got out of the van but stayed right by its door. My mother sat inside the van for a long time before I heard the door open, then close again behind her.

My mother was halfway down the path when she stopped and said, "Let's go home." Woo did not move from the side of the van.

I said nothing. I couldn't think of what to say. I felt as if there was nothing inside of me. Nothing at all. Not a thought, not a feeling, not a word. And I wanted to keep it that way. And keeping it that way depended on me staying right where I was, right on the porch, on the swing. Maybe forever.

"C'mon. Let's go home," my mother said again. She switched her keys from one hand to the other. "I'm going to drive you. Woo will meet us back home. If we leave now, I can get dinner on the table right on time."

She was not good at this kind of stuff. This parent-talking-to-a-kid stuff. I felt bad for her for a minute, and I started to get up; but things got all whirly and I clutched the swing's chain with one hand and white-knuckled the seat cushion with the other and was sure I was going to faint. Everything faded to whitish, but I could see that my mother was moving. She came down the rest of the path, but she did not come into the porch. She made the turn in front of the house and kept on walking. She was heading toward the other car, her car. My ears started to ring as she walked right in front of me. I saw her through the screen of the porch and the plastic on top of the screen that was meant to keep the winter at bay, so there was a warped, translucent grid between her and me. The ringing in my ears and weird brightness made everything creepy and dreamlike and hard to make out that she said to me, "I'll be in the car. You have five minutes."

... 8

Woo looks at the floor when he has to walk past me, so he won't have to make eye contact. I don't need to see his eyes to feel the fire that is there, the disappointment, the stony disapproval. He is furious. At me. Doug is, too; but at least Doug will look me in the eye once in a while. I see his weary pity for me.

My brother chose sides, and he did not choose mine.

I was born with my eyes locked onto my big brother. I followed him around and watched everything he did and wanted to do all those things myself. His name was Woo because I couldn't say "Will" when I first learned to talk. I couldn't say the letter *L*. He was the one who thought it was so adorable, the "Woo" thing. He made everybody call him that. He ignored it when stupid asshole kids said stupid asshole things to him, year after year, about him being Chinese like Hop Sing on the *Bonanza* show. They'd hold their palms together and bow, or they'd pull their eyes back into little slits with their fingers. He didn't care. He laughed and said, yeah, that was his name. Deal with it, jerk offs.

And now, it's like I am forced to watch as he gets into a car, locks all the doors, and drives farther and farther away while I just stand here.

Our after-school foursome broke up, of course. I am home by myself, like I am every day while my mother picks up my brother from his after-school stuff. The doorbell rings. The doorbell rings at 3:30 on a weekday afternoon, and I am sure to the marrow of my bones that it's Sean. I'm sure because Sean always hits the doorbell button twice in a row, with no pause in between, so the bell dingdongdingdongs in a manic blur.

My heart pounds. I have a hard time swallowing because there's a giant lump that's blocking my throat. Maybe Sean hasn't spotted me yet. I sit completely still, not moving a muscle, as if that can magically ensure that he won't be able to see me. I'm terrified to turn my head toward our front door, to possibly find myself directly in his line of vision, as he stands there. To see if his wild blue eyes have already locked onto me. I sit on the couch in our living room with my homework spread out around me. I had thought I was safe, safe in my own house on a Tuesday, midwinter day.

I stare at the living room curtains, floor-length, heavy old drapes, and I picture wrapping myself within them, smelling their delicious smell that enfolds all the smells of our family's cooking, pets, fireplace, fresh laundry, dirty socks. If only I can get to the drapes without Sean seeing me. I can envelop myself, clutch them in my hands, breathe them so deeply into my nostrils that—

The doorbell rings again, two more times.

Sean's face presses against the small glass pane of our door, squishing his nose and warping his features. He's staring directly at me. He has that wry half smile that used to stop me in my tracks and melt me into a heap. Jesus, that was four months ago. Four lifetimes ago.

My legs shake when I stand. I run my hands along my jeans as if I were smoothing a skirt, which is an inane and purposeless thing to do, but it buys me more time to hope my legs will be solidly beneath me and give me some degree of faith that I will be able to walk to the door. I clear my throat but have no confidence that I'll be able to utter sound, form words, *talk* when I need to.

My hand grabs the ancient glass doorknob. I don't turn it right away, as if I still believe I can prevent this scene from going any further. But the door is open, and Sean says, "Hey, I thought I'd hang out with your brother."

I nod. I feel like a complete idiot for being so scared.

But just for a split second.

Then I realize: Sean knows my brother isn't home. He knows Woo stays late after school. He knows that my mother goes to pick him up because there aren't any buses.

He knew I would be alone.

Sean moves as if to go past me. I am still standing in the doorway. My hand still clutches the glass knob. The winter day is so cold that the frigidity has travelled from the outside, through the length of the spindle as it slices through the door, to the glass touching my hand. I picture ice crystals forming on my fingertips, crawling up the length of my arm, and gamboling their way through me. The crystals freeze me solid. I am perfectly fixed in this instant, a blue version of me that dances with tiny, sparkling crystals like the inside of a windowpane on a subzero morning. I will never have to move or speak. Never, never.

Sean rocks back on his heel because I have not moved from the doorway. He is off-balance for a second, then gives my arm a shove and says, "I'll wait for him. That's fine."

That push was a little hard.

I wonder if I can move slowly enough—draw out each part of each movement—so my mother and Woo will be home by the time I have closed the front door. I check the mailbox, though of course my mother got the mail ages ago. I open the lid of our old milk box, which has not been used for years, and let its lid snap down. I kick my foot at the outdoor mat, as if the mat itself has an urgent need to be straightened; then I do the same with the inside mat, tugging at one corner to get it perfectly centered in front of the old wooden door. Sean sits on the living room couch, in the *exact spot* where I was sitting when he came to the door. He moved my books to the end table so he could sit there, so he could take over my spot. He looks at me with a neutral expression of idle curiosity, but smirks when he catches my eye. "Busy, busy," he says.

Go away go away go away go away, screams inside of me. Go away go away go away go away. I hear a car. My brother is driving. He always wants to drive. My mother chats away in the passenger seat. Sean says, "Sounds like your mom's car." I kneel on the front mat as if I'm praying. My face presses against the glass, and I watch my breath form foggy spots on the pane each time I exhale. It is a tremendous comfort, like water vapor condensing on glass is proof that the world is real and solid and predictable.

I can't tell what my mother is saying, can't make out the words, because it's more like she is singing a song. Her tone is light and lilting and carried way up high in her head, like an opera singer. She sings to Sean. She asks him if he wants cookies and milk. She has gone to the bakery earlier that day, she says, and they are fresh fresh fresh.

I hold myself back from breaking into a gallop up the stairs and into my bedroom. Even with my bedroom door closed and my music blasting, I hear a continuous melody of overly loud voices and laughter. My mother's high singing tones, the gravelly baritone of my brother, the slightly ironic twang of

Sean. I stare at the owl mobile that hangs from the light on my bedroom ceiling.

There are footsteps on the stairs, quick ones. My mother stands in my bedroom doorway. "Can't you at least be nice to him?" she says.

Why can't I just be nice to him?

I have a bad feeling about this, that's why.

I think about the time our dog Ilsa found a nest of baby bunnies up at the farm. When she poked her nose into their little burrow, the babies did their best to scatter. Ilsa zeroed in on one of them. She chased after it and scooped it up in her mouth, and in one quick, amazingly efficient movement, she broke its neck. Then she trotted back to the house with its limp little corpse, lay down in a patch of sun, and began to groom it.

My parents took the bunny away from her. They put Ilsa inside the house while they buried it deep in the woods. After a while, they let her outside again. A couple of hours later, Ilsa was back in her same place, her face and paws caked with dirt and leaves from unearthing the bunny. She licked it all over, trying to clean it off.

My parents built a fire. They held her collar and made her watch as they tossed the bunny carcass into the fire and let it burn. When they let go of her collar, she went into the flames. She poked in and out of the fire repeatedly, moving the bunny a little bit more each time, until she had removed it from the fire altogether. She trotted back to her spot while we all watched in shock and horror and awe.

Ilsa didn't want to eat it or harm it further in any way. She had claimed this bunny as her own. She wasn't going to give it up.

That's what I thought about Sean. That's what I thought he had done with me. He had claimed me in that same animal way.

● ● ●

"The most beautiful thing we can experience is the mysterious. It is the source of all true art and all science. He to whom this emotion is a stranger, who can no longer pause to wonder and stand rapt in awe, is as good as dead: his eyes are closed."

—Albert Einstein

Part II

Part II

...

And I know what he is doing here. I know.

I crouch down at the creek's edge and plunge my hands into the cool water. I spread my fingers wide, letting the creek's slow current flow over and around and between them. I turn my hands palm side up, raise them out of the creek, and watch the water run between my fingers.

Lula comes up behind me. She rests her hand on my shoulder to lower herself to the ground and sits beside me. Neither one of us says a word for a long, long time.

"Is Eddie all right, Lula?" I ask the same question a second time: "Is he all right?"

"He's not here, dear," Lula says.

"I'm not sure what I'm supposed to think," I say. "About that answer or about anything else." I can feel a single, silent tear making its way down my cheek. "Not sure at all." I keep saying the same things twice.

"When you told me what this place meant to you," Lula says, "—your treasured old family farm—you told me it was the place where there wasn't any 'supposed to.' There was just 'be.'"

"So, this is where my own words come back to haunt me?" I say. I am calm right now. My voice sounds reasoned, like I am asking a completely neutral question. "Gosh, I thought that didn't happen until you had children. I thought your kids were the ones who tossed your own words back at you."

"I suppose that's how it usually works," Lula says.

"But I didn't have children, did I, Lula?"

Lula says nothing.

"Sean killed me." I search Lula's face. She says nothing.

"It's all right; I figured it out. I died in the orchard. Sean killed me." I pause and think. "Which means that I'm dead, I think," I say. "I think that I must be dead."

...

Earlier.

... I

It's been a long time since I've stood on this porch. One of my favorite places in the world. I take two more steps to my left, and I am at the exact spot where I can see the farthest in three different directions. Two whole sides of the old farmhouse and the wraparound porch that encircles them. On the front section of the porch the black wooden swing hangs from the ceiling, a few of my grandmother's old throw pillows still strewn across the back. The creaky single bed with its blue-and-white embroidered cover—both there since my parents bought this place—takes up the far corner, keeping its lookout into the cave created by the copse of towering pines. The overflow bed, for times when we had more people visiting than would fit in the ten other sleeping places scattered throughout the house's four rooms. Or when it was so hot, so unbearably killingly humid, that Woo would opt to sleep on the porch. I never slept well when he did this. I missed him being in the other twin bed in our upstairs room. I felt betrayed.

Beyond the porch itself, through the slight muddy dimming from the screen's grid, a panoramic sweep of the land outside. Not all that much to see to the left, as the stone pathway leading from the porch door to the dirt road runs up a steep bank. I need to stoop down to get a glimpse of the road itself; otherwise the view is of a vertical slope, covered by a motley assortment of ferns and a couple of tenacious mountain laurel clinging to the incline and struggling to keep their grip and survive.

The springhouse is off to the right in its own little valley, with its eternal smell—a pungent mixture of creosote and gasoline and a million leftover pieces and parts of a million abandoned projects that have been there forever. Long before we got here. Useless tools, boxes of screws, cartons of nails, shotgun shell cases, gasoline cans, broken mousetraps, leaky hoses, pipe sections, caulk. We kept a combination lock on the rusty hasp of the springhouse door. I used to test myself each spring, after a whole winter of not coming here had gone by, to see if I could still remember the combination. But mostly, I was testing my fear. The springhouse was one of so many things that terrified me. I would open the combination lock, take off the old hasp, and see how many steps I could walk into the springhouse itself. I would stand there, just breathing the acrid air, looking at the relics that covered most of the floor space. Sometimes I would touch a couple of things. But mostly it was about standing there, forcing myself to face my own terror, maybe a few more seconds each year.

I relocked the hasp with enormous relief. Back outside. Free from the ghosts of so many discarded objects from times long gone. I would then descend the crumbling, mossy stone staircase that led to the spring itself, a little burble of water that was barely noticeable as it made its way out of its ground source deep below. Because of the spring, the area at the bottom of the stairs stayed as cold as a crypt. Woo and I would go down there on sultry summer afternoons and idle at the bottom of the stairs. The space was barely large enough for the two of us to stand together. It was too wet and slippery and mossy to even consider sitting down on the sharp rocky stairs; we'd linger and cool off until we were bored out of our minds and needed to escape back into the summer day.

That little burble provided the water for our farmhouse and fed a pond that my parents had dredged. In the early morning of a late winter day, the four of us gathered to watch two bulldozers creep their way down from the road and onto the hillside behind the springhouse. Their brilliant yellow stood out sharply against the gray of the sky and the rich brown of the earth. The dredgers worked nonstop for hours. The watery sun was nearly at its peak when one of the drivers signaled to the other. They drove the two bulldozers up the steep banks of the crater they had created, waved to our family, and drove off. The flow from the spring had already begun to fill the enormous hole, though at first it looked like a muddy, messy mistake. When the hole filled, we had a pond. Even a gentle breeze sent shimmery little waves of silver tickling across the surface. When the air was still, the olive-green water reflected the whole world surrounding our pond in perfect duplicate. We could stand on our floating dock and cast our fishing lines for sunfish and trout and perch. And crappies!—there was a kind of sunfish that was actually called a crappie, and Woo and I never tired of coming up with new jokes about crappie fish. Or we could jump from the dock into the cool water and splash around. I was always scared that the fish were going to bite me. If one of them got interested and followed me, I paddled back to the dock in a near panic, keeping a wary eye on the curious fish the entire time. I never stayed in the water for long. The springhouse was creepy and scary, but, altogether, it seemed safer than the pond as a way to cool off.

Not now, not in the height of summer, but in the spring, if I listened carefully from this very spot, I could hear the creek that lay just beyond the farthest edge of the field, at the very beginning of the trail into the woods. Full and ripe with the winter's runoff, the freezing water tumbling over the rocks in rushing abandon. I could hear it, even from such a distance, before it began its gradual evolution from bursting its muddy banks to flowing in a steady and patient stream, to trickling in ever-shifting paths between the mossy stones, to its eventual disappearance in the flush of summer. When I get a chance, I need to check the creek. Which I will always pronounce as "creek" rather than "crick" like most of the people from around here say it. I learned my lesson about that. I thought I was being nice and polite and friendly by saying "crick" when I was talking to the local folks. But the locals knew my family were weekend people. They thought I was making fun of them when I pronounced it "crick," and they'd get strangely quiet or, sometimes, outright mean. Such a point of contention. Makes me tired to think about it. How strong people's feelings can be about the strangest things. How people can assume the worst, right off the bat.

Anyway, here I am. On the porch. The whole day ahead of me. In the spot where I can see everything. The field, aflame with wildflowers. The orchard. I still think that was a ridiculous place to plant an orchard. Never for the life of me could figure out *why there,* the rockiest, craggiest, most inhospitable part of the whole farm. We always called it "Bishops' Orchard," named for the family who owned the farm before we did. It's almost certain that the roughhewn old trees had been planted well before the Bishops' tenure on this land. But it's always useful to have someone to blame, and we blamed the Bishops for the unreasonable location.

Wait. I swear there was movement back there. Way at the back of the orchard. It's too late in the morning for deer. Plus, why would a deer decide to stroll right through the open orchard? And it's too early in the summer for any of the fruit to have ripened and fallen.

Was that a flash of red?

I realize I have risen onto my tiptoes to get a better look. Either

57

that's the world's largest cardinal or...no, too high above the ground. That can only be a person. A person walking very, very slowly. Right through the middle of the orchard.

I am clutching the back of the chair at the porch table. The chair that my mother sat in—her place at the family table—the seat with the best view. I feel the heat rise in my cheeks, the feeling that the tops of my ears have caught fire. Well, there's somebody strolling right across our orchard, it seems. Why wouldn't I be scared? Or wary, at least. Let's say I'm wary. I strain to make sense of the colors and shapes that appear and disappear through the branches of the ancient apple trees. A full head of snow-white hair—it's an older person. A cotton print dress, a lot like the ones my grandmother and her sisters wore. A woman, then. That makes me feel a little better, I guess. White ankle socks. Well-worn walking shoes. A red bandana around her neck—the flash of red I saw when she was still at the far end of the orchard. Is that a walking stick? A cane? She is putting a lot of her weight on it, leaning heavily. She hasn't looked up. She can't. She needs to watch her feet intently, making her way among the multitude of rocks in the uneven, hazardous orchard.

She has made her way to the near end of the orchard, quite close to the old farmhouse, before she chances a glance upward. She immediately sees me standing behind the chair at the outdoor table, here on the porch, not twenty yards away.

She raises her cane in a kind of salute and calls out, "Oh! Hello, dear!" in a nonchalant, normal sort of way. Like this is an everyday thing that's happening.

I'm completely uncertain what to do or say, so I stick with a tentative, "Hello."

"I'm not used to seeing anyone!" the woman says. "You gave me rather a start."

I don't even think before blurting out, "It's my place," and add, "my family's place."

"Oh, I'm sure it is, dear, seeing as you're standing there on the porch. But I walk through here every day, through your orchard there."

What does she mean she walks through here every day? This is *our farm*. But I say, "I just got here. Last night." I feel an odd sense that I need to justify my own presence on my own porch.

"Never saw anyone here before. It's a bit startling," she says. She does seem startled and a little off-balance. But friendly. I would almost say sweet.

"It's been a while since I've been up here. Just got here last night," I say. "I guess I just said that, didn't I?" Well, that was just a wee tad awkward. "It's funny, right before I saw you I was just thinking about that orchard," I say. "Wondering why anyone would choose such rocky, uneven ground for an orchard in the first place." I'm generally not one to talk to strangers at all, let alone trespassers. There's something about her. Disarming. Welcoming. I'm not sure exactly.

"Well, I can't answer that one," she says, and she looks back over her shoulder at the orchard behind her, shielding her eyes from the morning sun like she's scanning the landscape for clues.

"What I'm wondering now is, why you would walk through such a dangerous orchard, when the road is right there?" I point.

"The road gets a bit tiresome after a while, lovely as it is. I do walk on it. This is my little foray off the beaten path, as it were. Just through your orchard and back on up to the road. It's one of the few places there's a break in the woods for quite a ways, you know."

"I do know. That's why my parents fell in love with this place. That's why they bought it. To get away from everything. Absolutely…everything." I am talking to a total stranger, who is technically trespassing on my old family farm. Quite a far cry from the usual me.

The woman smiles. I can't think of what to say.

"Oh. Perhaps you'd rather that I don't walk through it," the woman says.

I consider this. "Well, I'm not sure that makes much sense," I say. "Seems kind of mean-spirited and arbitrary, out here in the middle of all this *land*. And frankly, you don't seem to pose any kind of threat. No, you go right on walking through the crazy, rocky orchard any time you like."

"Very kind of you, dear. I suppose if you're up and about, I'll see you tomorrow."

I ask her if she walks this way every day and she says, "I do, indeed." I like that—the way she says "indeed."

"Where are you headed, anyway?" I ask her.

"That way." She points up the road, the opposite direction from where she came, as if that's a complete and proper explanation. She turns from me and makes her way up the path without another word.

...2

The next morning, I stand at the kitchen sink and fill the archaic aluminum coffeepot with water. I can see nothing outside the kitchen window. Nothing at all. I strain my eyes, but there is only a dense, gray nothingness. A pea-soup fog. That's what they call it in this neck of the woods—a pea-soup fog. I have not seen a fog of its like in a long while.

It's as if the house has no outside walls. They fade and bleach into nonexistence, vanishing into the gray. Fog as thick as this drinks up all sound, except for the occasional plops of water —the humidity so high that droplets condense out of thin air and fall heavily to the ground. It makes me think of being in an airplane, flying through an impenetrable cloud bank, surrounded by an utter void, feeling as if I am being propelled deeper and deeper into nothing at all.

I may not be able to see the elderly woman when she comes walking through the orchard today. Or, the woman may well decide to bypass the orchard altogether, as she would not be able to see the treacherous rocks endangering her path. In this kind of fog, people and things appear out of nowhere, without hint or warning, when they come close enough to emerge from the fog's grip. They disappear just as fast.

It's strange. I just met the old woman—if you can even call that a "meeting"—and I feel like I don't want to miss her if she takes her walk today. Maybe I'll just wander about a little while I'm drinking my coffee, check the orchard, take a peek up the road. I hold the screen door and close it gently behind me, careful to make no sound. The door's usual slam seems like it would be an improper intrusion into this silent, featureless world. I wander the short distance to the near end of the orchard, where the ancient apple trees appear out of the gray, one by one. I run my hand along the craggy bark, run my finger in the grooves between the bark's scales.

I take a couple more steps into the orchard. On one of the low, jagged rocks, I make out the faint remains of white paint. Even in dim and fog, the old paint produces a chiaroscuro of light and dark in the deep crags. My father painted a number of rocks throughout the orchard, a warning for himself and anyone else driving one of our ride-on lawn mowers through the obstacle-course orchard. I adored our two ride-on lawn mowers. The first one we got, which was smaller and slower than the second, remained my favorite. Much as I loved to ride on Snapper—my pet name for the little red mower—I never mowed the apple orchard, never wanted to try. But my father approached it as a challenge, a game, to see how fast he could go, careening around, turning sharp corners, timing himself. I can picture him in his perennial, enduring work outfit—a plain white T-shirt and light blue pants—perched high up on the mower with a whisper of a smile on his face. He hit various rocks many, many times. I will never forget the sound. The noisy, constant engine halting in an instant, giving way to the thunderous scrape of metal against rock that seemed to shake the surrounding woods to their core, then stopping dead in abrupt silence.

One time was different. The metallic crash was not met by silence, but by the continuing whirr of the engine and, within that sound, my father's screams. "Help! Help me!" I had never heard panic in his voice before. On one of his daredevil sharp corners, the mower had tipped over—completely on top of him—and the blades kept on turning.

I'm not sure why a shudder just went through me. Once we got the motor stopped and the mower lifted off of him, he was fine. Not a scratch. Must be a worse memory than I thought, though, because my stomach hurts. I want to get out of the orchard. Right now.

I wander back to the house and climb the path to the road. I feel better already. I take my time, looking in both directions for long intervals, in case the old woman decided to walk on the road. If she comes through the orchard, I will see her from here anyway.

There is a slight movement at the farthest edge of visibility that the fog allows. It vanishes. I continue to watch for a long while, but there is nothing more. Just me on a dirt road surrounded by nothing at all. It may have been the woman. There is no way to be sure.

…3

There is not one cloud in the sky this morning. The sun dazzled the first moment it burst over the horizon. It doesn't seem possible that this could be the same world as the one where the fog sucked everything out of sight.

The morning dew, heavy on each individual blade of grass, lights up into a sea of sparkle as millions of dewdrops reflect the sun's rays. I open the screen door, and this time I let it slam in its completely familiar, exhilarating slam. I need to feel the carpet of wet grass on my bare feet. I kick my foot hard into the grass, sending a fountain of droplets into the air. I watch the arcs of their ascents and falls. The power of the sun combined with the chill of the dew sends a thrill through my entire body. The eerie silence of yesterday has been displaced. The forest has erupted into raucousness. Birds seem to have swelled their volume in jubilant reverence of the day's beauty. A spider has spun a vast web in one short morning. Its strands run from the hinge on the porch door to the nearest bush—easily four feet away—and each of the slender threads glistens with dewdrops. For the infinitude of things that scare me, I was never afraid of walking smack-dab into a spiderweb. It's a strange feeling to have your face unexpectedly wrapped in delicate, slightly sticky strands, but I always considered it a kind of magic, an omen of good luck.

I kick once again into the grass, and when I look up to watch the droplets spray into the air, there is the older woman, walking stick in hand, watching me from the nearest edge of the orchard, no more than twenty feet away.

I feel caught in a private moment, and I try to cover it. I work for nonchalance and say, "Oh, hey! Hey there! Hello... sorry, I don't know your name."

"Lula, dear. My name is Lula," she says. If she thinks I may have been acting peculiar, nothing reveals it. She is as open as the day itself.

I say, "Holy cow, my mother had an aunt Lula—my great-aunt. I've never heard of anyone else with that name."

"Well, it was actually a rather common name way back when. Sometimes short for Luella, sometimes for Lucretia. Even Louise and Talullah often got shortened to Lula." She taps her walking stick–cane against the bottoms of her shoes to knock off clumps of dirt. She adjusts her hat—she's wearing a hat today, an old, frayed one that looks for all the world like it should have fishing lures hanging from the band, and she says, "Funny enough, my name isn't any of those. It's Eulalia."

Somehow this tickles me to an inordinate degree, and I gush, "Eulalia! That's *beautiful!* I've never known *anyone* named Eulalia!"

"Oh, I'm glad you like it, dear," she says. "Can't say that I was ever nearly as excited as you seem to be. Not that I ever heard anyone call me that. I was Lula ever since I can remember."

"Now I have a name for you. Something besides 'the older woman who walks through my orchard.'" I'm pretty sure that sounded exceptionally weird, maybe even offensive. I say, "I'm not sure if I can call you that—Lula, I mean. Sometimes we just can't stray too far from the ways that we were raised. My parents would faint if I called an older person—a person who was older than me—I hope I'm not offending you…my parents would die if I called you 'Lula.'"

"Are they here, dear?" She feigns craning her neck and does a quick exaggerated scan of the surrounding area. "I hadn't seen them."

Like I said, she has a disarming, gentle solidness. I laugh. "No. I'm all alone here. Just me."

"Then I think you should call me Lula, short for Eulalia, and I should call you…?"

"Mazie," I say. "Just Mazie. Not short for anything."

"I am delighted to make your acquaintance, Mazie. I imagine I may see you tomorrow," Lula says.

I'm a bit taken by surprise at the soon-to-be abrupt departure. "Oh, off on the rest of your walk, are you?" I ask her.

She has already turned her back when she waves her walking stick and heads up the path. She turns back to me and says, "I suppose I should carry my own, but might I trouble you for a glass of water next time? Should we see one another again?"

"Let me get you one right now," I say as I prepare to hurry inside and fetch her a glass.

But as I walk toward the door to the kitchen, I see that Lula has continued up the path. She is nearly at the road, already out of sight except for the bottoms of her legs and her worn-out shoes.

...4

I stand on the porch, holding a tall glass filled to the brim with water and ice. Waiting for Lula. I don't even make a pretense of being anything less than intrigued—and eager—to see her again.

When she raises her cane in greeting, I say, "I have some ice-cold water for you here. Are you in a hurry? Would you like to sit down and rest a minute?"

"I don't believe I'm ever in a hurry," she says.

"I've been accused of that," I say. "More than a time or two. Come in and have a seat, if you'd like."

I hold the porch door open for her. She walks over to the

table with its four chairs and chooses the one that I used to sit in the whole time Woo and I were growing up. I put the water down in front of her and say, "I got gypped, Lula. That was my place at the table, the chair you're sitting in."

Lula sits forward as if to move and says, "Oh, I'm sorry, dear. I didn't mean to sit in your chair."

I feel awful for bringing it up. "No, no," I say. "It's the only seat without a view. That's what I meant about feeling gypped." I worry that sounds whiny and bitter, and I add, "I'm kidding." Except I'm not kidding, not entirely. I say, "Well, I'm kind of kidding. It's a funny thing."

Lula drinks heartily, almost the entire tumbler in one long gulp, and says, "What's that, dear? What's a funny thing?"

"It's funny how things get decided in families. Like who sits where. Who knows how that happened? I'm pretty sure there's wasn't a single word exchanged. But once it happened, once we all sat down on a certain chair, those became our PLACES. For the rest of time. Me, facing the door into the kitchen, my back to the whole wide world."

"I've been on my own for...oh, pretty much forever," Lula says. "But I do know what you mean."

"Forever is a long time," I say. She takes another long drink and doesn't say anything. I worry that maybe I sounded sarcastic or insensitive or, most likely, just plain lame. I feel like I need to fill in the gap. The first thing that pops into my mind is, "We were a family of game players. Cardplayers, mostly. And you know, whenever we gathered to play cards, we'd always sit in our exact same places at the table! Like I said, I was gypped!" I don't even feel it coming. A genuine, unfettered laugh springs from way inside of me, like something that has been asleep is beginning to awaken.

"You were cardplayers?" Lula asks me.

"Holy cow, yes," I say. "I was born into it. No choice, really."

"I dearly love a good card game!" Lula rubs her hands together, absentmindedly, but like she thoroughly relishes the idea. It's charming. "Why, I don't know how you're spending your time while you're up here," she says, "but if you'd be interested in a hand or two…sometime…"

"Sure!" I say.

"Gin rummy is my personal favorite. Do you know gin rummy, Mazie?"

This time it's a belly laugh. "I'm pretty sure there isn't a card game for two, three, or four people that I don't know. Well, euchre. I have no idea how to play that one. Otherwise, I'm your gal."

"Wonderful," she says.

"I'm warning you that I play for fun. Meaning I'm not the competitive, cutthroat type. Meaning I'm not like my parents. They would discuss specific bridge hands for *days* after they played them. Days! They'd remember every card. They'd discuss all the different possibilities for how the hand could have been played. It was like listening to people speaking a foreign language. I could sit right there with them and not understand a single word, but I'd be fascinated by the tones, the inflections. They would be *so excited.*" I laugh again. "I always thought of myself as such a weird little kid, but maybe it wasn't all me." That felt like too much, too soon. I find myself genuinely liking Lula, feeling drawn to her, and because of this I am trying too hard. I try to cover my tracks. "Anyway, gin rummy. Anytime, Lula. Anytime."

...5

Lula says, "Good morning dear," as she opens the screen door and steps up to the porch. She seems particularly light; she has the proverbial pep in her step. I see that she is holding one arm behind her back. She brings the arm forward and says, "I brought you some flowers I picked along the way. Thought it would brighten our table to have a nice centerpiece while we played our gin rummy." Lula holds out a bunch of wildflowers on long stems, stunning little orange and yellow spotted blooms that look like tiny orchids.

"Oh my God, they're *beautiful!*" I say.

"Watch," Lula says. She reaches out a single finger and touches what looks like a green pea pod attached to the end of one of the stems. With Lula's barest touch, the seedpod bursts apart, and shoots of curly green confetti race in all directions.

I gasp, then laugh. "Oh my gosh. I'd forgotten all about these flowers!"

"Aren't they a marvel?" she says.

"I used to *love* these!" I gush, without self-consciousness. "I remember when my brother and I discovered them. The orchard was filled with them! They appeared out of nowhere. I can't even remember which one of us—my brother Woo or me—accidentally touched one of the seedpod things while we were looking at the flowers, and BOOM an explosion of…crazy seeds, right? Crazy seeds disguised as tiny party streamers! We spent the whole afternoon combing through the orchard and popping the seedpods. A whole afternoon. When we'd found every single one, we lay down on the ground, head-to-head, staring up at the clouds and making up stories about their shapes. Woo chewed on long stems of timothy grass. He had on his favorite striped T-shirt, jeans that were a little too short, white socks, and penny loafers. It was his penny loafer phase. He wore them everywhere, all the time." I feel suddenly serious when I tell Lula, "That was a great, great day."

"It's called jewelweed. People sometimes call it orange jewelweed or spotted jewelweed." Lula pulls out her chair and tells me, "The common name for it is touch-me-not. You can see why."

"We didn't have any idea what they were. My mother didn't know either, which nearly gave us heart attacks, as she generally knew everything. Woo and I looked for them every year, but I don't remember ever finding them again." I turn another degree more serious, but in a good way, and add, "Never finding them again made that one afternoon seem all the more like some kind of...magic."

"Oh, wildflowers do seem to have minds of their own. They appear here and there and disappear. But it's *Impatiens capensis,* not magic," Lula sighs a big, contented sigh as she sits.

"It's what?" I ask her.

"That's the Latin name for the plant—*Impatiens capensis.*"

"You're starting to remind me of my mother. She knew a lot of things about a lot of things, too," I say.

"The juice from the stems and leaves has long been used for itching—going back ages. It can actually stop poison ivy from getting bad if you rub the juice on right away. I've even heard tell that it can clear up ringworm and athlete's foot as well," Lula draws a circle in the air when says "ringworm" then reaches down and taps her shoe with her index finger when she mentions athlete's foot.

"Now you're really reminding me of my mother. When I was little, I was convinced she had to be making stuff up—no one could really have such an encyclopedic knowledge of so many different things. Later on, Woo and I used to tease her that she got some kind of secret newsletter that was filled with random tidbits of information, and she would memorize every bit of it while we were at school, just waiting for a chance to throw in some new tidbit of knowledge."

"Everybody around here knows about ol' jewelweed," Lula says. She shrugs her shoulders and raises her hands beside them—palms up—while looking up to the heavens. The gesture strikes me as so unique, so entirely her own, that I feel something akin to butterflies in my stomach. Her shrug divulges wonder, innocence, and irony all at once. I worry that I may tear up.

"'Everyone around here' just happens to know the Latin name?" I ask her.

"Oh, well, I suppose not," Lula says. "Now that you mention it." She gives me a wry smile that seems charmingly enigmatic and coy. "How about we put these beauties in some water and play some cards?"

"Thank you for bringing jewelweed, Lula. Thank you for reminding me of one of the very best days I ever had." I take the flowers from her hand, and I swear I can feel it—lying on the ground in the orchard, head-to-head with Woo, staring up at the clouds. The bristles of his buzz cut pressing into my scalp at the point where our heads touch. Little flyaway strands of my hair blow across my field of vision and brush my cheeks. The towering stalk of his timothy grass chew waves back and forth as he moves it around with his teeth. My eyes fill, and I tell Lula that I need to go to the kitchen to get a vase for the flowers. The jewelweed.

I return with an old milk-glass vase filled with water and put it on our table. Lula shuffles the deck of cards that I had gotten out. I put the flowers in their vase and watch her old hands adeptly handle the shuffling. There is something that seems perfect about those hands. "Don't you think it's amazing that my brother and I only found them that one year?" I ask her. "I spent a lot of time wandering around looking for them. We used to come up here pretty much every weekend from the time the snow melted in the spring until the time it started up again in the fall. And after all this time, here they are again."

Lula doesn't respond. She seems focused on the cards and the thought of the game ahead. Lula pushes the cards toward me and says that we should cut the deck to determine who deals. I draw the ten of spades. Lula draws the nine of clubs, and I deal out the hands. I'm a little afraid that I'm talking her to death, but I say, "Do you know what? These cards were here when we bought this farm. The Bishops—the people who owned this place before my family did—just walked out one day, and we walked in. They left everything. *Everything!* Like a neutron bomb had gone off. Every sign of human life had vanished; every remnant and relic stayed behind. The kitchen cabinets were filled with their dishes. The drawers held their silverware, their cooking utensils, their potholders. Towels hung on the towel racks. Freshly washed sheets lay carefully folded in the upstairs bureaus. Extra ones, because all five of the beds had sheets and blankets and pillows already on them, carefully arranged. They left their board games, their decks of cards, even their jigsaw puzzles with a piece or two missing, in an old oak table. I used to go around each room of the farmhouse, opening every drawer and looking at the things inside. It was as if my family had walked into someone else's life. I mean, look at these cards! At some point in history, somebody went into a store somewhere and looked through all the decks of playing cards, and they picked these—the ones with the Grecian urns overflowing with fake grapes. One deck with a watery purple background, the other deck a muted peach. Someone thought these extremely odd cards were the *perfect thing*. And here we are, two people who were complete strangers just a few days ago, who met by chance, now playing a game of gin rummy with those very cards, so many years later."

"Two people who at some point may play gin rummy," Lula says. "Or may not."

"Point taken. Your turn," I say.

"How did your family pass the time when you all came up here?" Lula asks me.

"Oh, well, my parents had an endless and eternal number of Projects they were dying to work on. Fix the fence, cut back the raspberry bushes, mow the grass, trim the fruit trees in the orchard, switch out the rotting planks on the side of the barn, fix the fence again. They worked all day long—worked like dogs. I could never understand the appeal of buying a second home that seemed to me like a ceaseless amount of work. And a pressure. If we had to miss a weekend for some reason they would *worry*, as if entropy's pull was so powerful that the whole place would tumble into chaos without constant work. Everything was a 'supposed to'—they were supposed to fix, repair, cut back, mow, build, take down. It took me a long time to figure out that their way of enjoying the place was to *work on it*. They had to have their hands dug into it—deeply and physically—in order to enjoy it.

"It couldn't have been more different for me. This was the place, the one place, where there was no 'supposed to,' Lula. Just *be*. That has always been the very best thing about this place. It's as if…the whole rest of the world just falls away. The 'real world,' I mean. All of the…jumble of bits and pieces that rattles around in our heads. All of the expectations about *how* we're supposed to be, *who* we're supposed to be, those kinds of things. It's stripped-down here. Like I said. No 'supposed to.'"

Lula has not even picked up her cards. She seems to be waiting to hear what I have to say. I look out across the expanse of land and say, "Sometimes I just need to be here. Need to. Like now."

...6

The next morning, I find myself on the porch again. I hand Lula a glass of water. Again. I sit down in the chair where my mother used to sit. The deck of cards sits on the corner of the table, and I begin to shuffle, making bridges and watching the old cards fall together in beautiful, slow motion. Old cards are always easiest to shuffle. It's as if they remember; they understand what they're supposed to do. I deal ten cards each to Lula and myself, and, just like that, I start talking. I tell her that the whole reason we bought this old farm was because of the sole family vacation we took—a road trip all the way across the country, when I was four years old. A cross-country trip in the family station wagon to visit my aunt and uncle and the new baby cousin in California. West along old Route 66 from Pennsylvania to California. Four interminable, dreary states just to hit Route 66 in the first place, which didn't end up looking any less dreary than the four states that came before we reached our entry point somewhere in Illinois.

First and last family road trip.

Days and days of endless barren landscapes, our spanking new station wagon throwing up a dust storm that followed in our wake. No air conditioning. The windows were wide open, making any kind of talking sort of impossible. It was dry and dusty, with a hot wind blowing in our faces all day long. My brother and I bounced and blew around in the back seat in a woozy stupor. Every so often, one of us would come out of our haze long enough to let out a plaintive whine of "how much longer?" or, even more important, "are you sure there's a POOL?"

I was pretty sure my parents were tricksters, I say to Lula. I'm surprised to find myself saying this. It's a big thing to confess—what a weird and suspicious little kid I was. But it's true. From an early age, I was watching them out of the corners of my eyes.

Lula says, "Maybe you just noticed things."

I'm not exactly sure what she means by that, but I'm on a roll, a speed rap, as my husband Eddie used to say, and I plunge on, saying: I got to eat pancakes every morning. Which was unheard of at home. At one of the pancake places, I got a stuffed burro with a bright, shiny red collar around his neck and a little leash attached to the collar. He also had a bell inside of his ear. He was my special souvenir of the trip. Except I wasn't allowed to make the bell ring in the car because it drove everyone nuts, or in the motel rooms either, so mostly I just held him in my lap and stared at him. He looked kind of sad and flea-bitten, really, but I loved him. I sat in the back of the station wagon and petted him and fooled with his collar for the last thousand miles.

The new baby was my cousin, they said. It was a miracle, they said, because my aunt had tried so hard to have a baby and wanted one so much. They told me that she had lost fifteen babies, which I found completely confusing but nonetheless terrifying. How could anyone lose babies? The idea made me feel cagey about my aunt, and I guess my mother sensed this because she kept reminding me that I loved my aunt very much, as was evidenced by the fact that I didn't shy away from her for even a single second when she stuck her finger down my throat and made me upchuck because I had eaten cockroach poison. That was during our previous visit to my aunt and uncle. I was less than two years old; I didn't know what I was doing. I just figured that something lying on the floor in a pretty little bowl was something I should definitely taste. Of course, I have no memory of this myself, being so young at the time, but my mother told that story so many times that it's like a movie that can play in my mind at the merest mention. I can picture my aunt's pin curls flopping in front of her eyes as she held me over the sink. I can smell the smell of her breath combined with the fragrance of her bright lipstick as she panted with effort. I guess I didn't upchuck all that easily, which was all part of the story of my good nature in not holding an immense grudge against someone who hoisted me under her arm and forced her finger into the back of my throat over and over.

When we finally got to California, everything looked too bright to me. It seemed as if the whole world had been bleached into an eerie whiteness; I was scared of a sun that seemed to have faded all color into a washed-out, pale sea. It didn't seem like it could possibly be safe to go outside, and I even made sure to keep clear of the windows at midday.

My aunt and uncle had recently moved into a new house and had practically no furniture. There were a seemingly endless number of empty, freshly carpeted rooms with nothing but a baby toy or a dog bone, strewn here and there. They also had a nervous little dog named Pierre that looked like he'd been given much too tight of a permanent wave for his hair. Pierre would continually get underfoot, and my uncle would swear at him then snicker and pretend that he hadn't sworn or yelled at the dog at all.

As for the baby cousin: I'd pretty much never seen a baby before and I wasn't at all sure she was real. She sat there doing absolutely nothing most of the time. Every so often I would pinch her to see if she was real after all. She would scream or cry or something, but I still wasn't entirely convinced.

I was scared of the people who lived next door, fretted that they were really, really bad and dangerous and would snatch me up or hurt me if I got too close to them. They were always trying to get me to come over to their gate to talk to them or to show me something. They didn't speak English! The adults kept trying to explain to me that they spoke Portuguese, came from a faraway country called Portugal, and had been fishermen. I understood that this was somehow supposed to be comforting, but it didn't have that effect at all. The old couple wore clothes that covered them all up from head to toe, and they were older than even my grandparents. I made sure never to get too close to that gate, even if I didn't see the old people milling about in their yard. But avoiding the gate meant that I had to stay inside my aunt and uncle's garage and that was terrifying, too! My aunt had shown me a little glass bottle on the garage shelf that she swore had a real genie inside of it. It looked empty, but my aunt was a doctor—a pediatrician, in fact—so it didn't make sense to me that she would lie to little kids. It was hard to find a place in the garage that was far enough from the gate and from the genie bottle, both. But at least I could stand there and shake my burro's bell as much as I wanted.

My parents seemed to think that everything was funny. They laughed all the time in California, and I was fairly sure they were laughing at me. But I was watching them. They just seemed like people with a lot of secrets. Mean people. With secrets. "See what I mean?" I say to Lula, "weird, suspicious little four-year-old. My aunt. The elderly people next door. My own parents. I was worried and scared about everyone."

I stop talking and I look at Lula. She smiles at me. "Go on, dear," she says.

"Lula," I say to her, "I'm not exactly sure how I got here."

"You were telling me about your trip to California. You'd just gotten to the part where you finally reached your aunt and uncle's house, and you could play with your little burro."

I feel like the world around me has gone out of focus. I clear my throat. I take a big gulp of the ice-cold water, and I feel the chill descend every inch of my chest as the liquid makes its way down. "That's not exactly what I meant when I said—"

But Lula interrupts me. "Go on, dear," she says. She reaches out her hand, and she puts it on top of mine. She squeezes my hand once. I clear my throat and go right back to talking.

I tell her that my aunt and uncle decided they wanted to rent a boat while we were visiting. They wanted to go out into the open ocean, they said. They wanted to take everyone out on the boat so they could go fishing for yellowtail. The grown-ups talked about this for DAYS beforehand—how we were going out into the open ocean, on our very own boat. They would look at one another every so often and shout out, "*Yellowtail!*", which was invariably followed by raucous laughter, back slapping, and big giant gulps from their tumblers.

When the much-vaunted day came, we set out for the place where the boat was docked. My aunt's car was so big that the accumulated seven of us had no trouble whatsoever fitting in. Even with three kids and one adult, we still bounced around the back seat with tons of space to spare. It was like being in a room in someone's house that up and moved from place to place. Riding in it didn't feel like any car I'd ever been in. When we drove over a bump in our family's station wagon, we'd feel

85

a bump. In this behemoth, when we went over a bump, the entire car seemed to take it personally and became intent on minimizing the blow by rolling from side to side a whole lot of times instead of just hitting the bump and getting it over with. When I looked over at my brother, the freckles across his nose had taken on a greenish tinge.

He got carsick a lot, even on regular old roads in a regular old car, I say to Lula.

The car's seats were made of a weird material that felt slippery and a little greasy all at the same time. I couldn't stop running my index finger back and forth across the seat beside me. My mother turned around from her spot in the middle of the front seat and caught me doing this. "It's a brand new synthetic!" she chirped. "It'll last *forever!*" Being four years old, I heard it as "SIN-thetic." And since I had a limited but wholly terrifying idea of "sin," and since my mother seemed unreasonably gleeful about the whole car upholstery topic, I decided that it was better to sit there in muddled silence than to say anything more. I felt that way quite a bit of the time, as a matter of fact.

When we climbed on to the actual boat, the adults were in such unfettered good spirits that I felt immediately suspicious and bewildered and like I'd been invited to some party that was celebrating something I couldn't understand. Plus, it turned out that you have to spend a whole lot of time on a boat, doing one thing and another that was also incomprehensible to me, way before the boat ever moves away from its place at the dock. But that whole time, the boat sits in the ocean heaving up and down and back and forth. Somebody decided that we children would be more comfortable "below." So, we—my aunt and the baby, my brother, and me—were relegated to the little enclosed room below the part of the boat that was outside and open to the air. Between the car ride and the bobbing up and down, I guess my brother wasn't feeling so very good, because the minute the little boat door closed, Woo did a quick look around, spotted a tiny little bench alongside a tiny little table, curled up, and immediately went to sleep.

I didn't know what to do—where to sit or stand or what to look at or anything. My aunt was holding the baby and cooing at her. That baby looked right at me, staring a hole. And without so much as a fuss or wiggle or even slight change of expression, she just opened up her mouth and spewed a gigantic amount of puke that ran all the way down her body and my aunt's body as well.

My aunt had a mess on her hands, and she got very wrapped up in wiping at the baby and herself with whatever she found nearby, all the while cooing and comforting her. Then the baby upchucked again.

I looked at my shoes. Partly because I still couldn't figure out what to do, and partly because I thought the puke probably splattered onto them. I was very proud of my saddle shoes and tried really hard to keep them looking brand new.

What the heck were my parents up to that they shut us away down here? I stared at the door to make sure I'd see them coming, whenever they did.

When I said that last bit to Lula, I swear I was right there, right on that boat. I could see the walls of the cabin heaving up and down; I could smell the faint trace of salty air mixed with baby puke and the strong odor of the thick coats of varnish on the boat's wood. But now I feel ashamed, self-conscious, about being such a serious and scared and kind of creepy little kid. I'm back on the porch. I take a big drink from my water glass and look through the porch screen to the orchard. Little green apples have started forming on the trees.

"You know what, Lula?" I say. "I don't remember eating a single apple from that orchard that tasted good. Ever. With all the different trees and all the different varieties of apples—not a single one, not one that you could pick off the tree and take a big bite out of and really like it."

"You don't say," Lula rearranges several of the cards in her hand without looking up.

"My mother fed them, sprayed them, pruned them, read books about them, and fussed over them. In the end, we made gigantic amounts of applesauce every fall. Even pies made with those apples weren't so great." I feel awkward and pissed off for no reason at all. I say, "Seriously, they tasted like shit." And then I feel like shit. Maybe Lula hates swearing. Maybe she's decided I'm a motormouthed, foulmouthed, suspicious-if-not-paranoid creep. Maybe she won't come back. I want her to come back, so I let her win the game. And the next one, too.

She pushes her chair back. She's getting ready to leave. I'm genuinely anxious that she may not return. "Lula, here's the thing. When we got back from that trip, I had a dream. I died. In the dream. But I thought that I really had. Died, that is." I hate myself for my naked attempt to reel her in, to make her interested enough to come back again tomorrow.

Lula says, "You don't say," again. Second time she's said it in as many minutes. And she says it as if it's the most mundane thing that she's ever heard, or pretty near it. "When I come back tomorrow, I'll look forward to hearing more."

"You don't say!" I know I'm being mean…mocking, and Lula looks at me like I've wounded her. "That's the exact same thing you said when you left the other day: 'when I come back tomorrow, I'll look forward to hearing more.' Exact. Same. That's a little weird!"

To my surprise, Lula laughs. "Never said I wasn't a little weird, Mazie. Never said. Aren't all the best folks a little weird, after all?"

...7

I open my eyes to the barest hint of daylight. It's more a shift in the spectrum from blue-black to gray-black than a change in the actual light. I stretch to my full length, luxuriating in what feels to me like an absolutely enormous double bed. When Woo and I were kids, we slept in the twin beds on the other side of this same upstairs bedroom. I usually slept in the one closer to the window that faces the front of the house. But unlike our permanent places at the porch table, every so often Woo and I would switch it up and sleep in the other bed. We never went upstairs together; there was only one rudimentary bathroom, down in the terrifying basement. We had to take turns brushing our teeth and doing all the sundry pre-bedtime routines. Whichever one of us came upstairs first would simply choose a bed for the night. Woo and I never talked about it, but I knew it was a fun game for both of us. The first one of us upstairs got the choice, and the second one got the surprise.

I am the only one here now, and I have chosen to sleep in the double bed that my aunt used when she visited the farm. If she wasn't here, the bed remained empty. We honored her unspoken but permanent claim on it. The only other time I've slept in this bed was when Eddie and I got married.

I pull the light summer quilt all the way to my chin, relishing the cool of the morning, the final moments before the temperature and humidity begin to soar. Before the cozy bedding sticks distressingly to every square inch of my body.

The double bed sits next to the room's other window, the one at the back of the house. When I turn my head to gaze out, I face the wide field. A coating of humidity blankets the whole area, a layer of mist that covers the first foot or so above the ground. It begins to dissipate so slowly, still hugging the ground, keeping its hold on the earth in the same way that I savor the bed's covers. At the far edge of the field, at the abrupt demarcation between the clearing and the woods, two deer stand at the salt lick. They take turns. There is plenty of room for both of them to lick the big salt block at the same time, but they take turns. When one deer looks up, the other one bends down. I creep out of bed as carefully as I can and kneel by the open window to watch. I slowly lower my head to rest my chin on the windowsill. I am far enough away in an unlit room that the deer would be unlikely to notice my movements, but I don't want to take a chance. I don't move a muscle. I want to savor the time. I watch them continue their elegant dance of moving heads—one up, the other down; one down, the other up—until the mist that had covered their legs has nearly vanished.

I begin to worry that Lula may come by on her walk and not see me on the porch, but I can't bear to tear myself away from the bedroom window. Not yet. I may never again see a scene of such serene and uncomplicated beauty. It's possible I'm avoiding Lula, I suppose. I did tell her the entire story of my life yesterday. How in the world did that happen? Then, after my long-running monologue, I got scared that I might have scared her away. Then I got mean because I'd gotten scared. Banner day, even for me.

Mere seconds before the sun breaks over the horizon, the two deer raise their heads at the same time, look at one another, turn their backs, and walk leisurely into the woods. It seems like a miracle to me.

When I make my way downstairs and open the kitchen door to the fresh morning air of the porch, I am taken aback to see that Lula is seated at the table. "Oh, I was thinking I might miss you today," I say. "I was watching two deer. I hope you haven't been waiting long."

"I saw them. The deer," she says. "Haven't been waiting that long at all."

"You saw them? You saw them, and you didn't scare them away?" I ask her. This is baffling. If she had walked through the orchard, her movement surely would have startled them. They would have flashed their beautiful white tails and bounded for the safety of the woods.

"The deer and I have an understanding, you could say." Lula smiles. "I did get to thinking—about understandings—and I have to say, Mazie, that I'm fairly certain you were letting me win at cards yesterday. If I'm right about that, I suggest we have an understanding ourselves, you and me. Play your hand. Play it to your best, and I will, too." Lula shuffles the cards and adds, "In cards as in life, it's the only way to go."

"Oh, geez," I say, "if you're going to wax philosophical or whatever, I'm going to make an extra-large pot of coffee." We're joking with one another. A détente has been reached. The pique and hurt feelings and embarrassment of the previous day have evaporated, like so much morning mist. Lula and I like one another again.

I know that Lula wants to hear about the dream, or maybe I just think she wants to hear about it because I want to tell it. I pour each of us a cup of coffee from the ancient pot. I explain to her that it started with the whole Grand Canyon thing, on our trip home from California.

Since it's a gruelingly long, dust-bitten journey slouching our way back toward Pennsylvania, my parents decide we should stop at some natural wonders along the way. Death Valley. Joshua Tree. The Painted Desert. My mother sits in the front seat and continually scans the landmark scenery with hawklike vigilance. She wears sunglasses, very dark green ones, so I can never see her eyes, not one bit, no matter how hard I try. Plus, wearing glasses always makes my mother hold her mouth funny, like a snarling upper lip is essential to keep the glasses in place. Her back is straight as a stick, her mouth is screwed up, and her head moves back and forth until—every so often—she shoots her hand out to graze my father's arm and yells, "Stop the car!" Doesn't matter how many times she does this, my brother and I rocket out of our back-seat stupor into a fit of instant panic.

She sounds enthusiastic, but we all know it's a command. My father pulls the car over to the side of the road too fast, sending up a spray of gravel and dust so my mother is sure to know that he's pissed. She ignores him. The second the car comes to a full stop, she leaps out the door and slams it hard behind her. Then she stands there, by the car, with her hands planted on her hips and her feet wide apart, surveying the scene, planning her attack. Around her neck hangs her regular camera, and wrapped tight around her wrist is the thin, worn shoelace cord of her wind-up, 8mm movie camera.

It always seems to take her a minute to remember the other three of us. Then she swings her body around and looks at my brother and me still sitting in the back seat as if the folly of our remaining in the car is beyond comprehension. Her face goes from disbelief to annoyance, and when it starts to turn the corner past annoyance, my brother and I get out of the car and shuffle along behind her, slowly, willful in our disinterest.

My father gets out, too, but he stays right by the car. He lights a cigarette, rests his arms on the car roof, and smokes. He makes all of this look like it's a great chore, a burden, but one that must be done.

My mother knows a lot about a lot, or says she does, which, like I told you, Lula, makes me suspicious. How can you go to so many different places, and the same one person knows so much about all the trees and the flowers and the cactuses and the birds and on and on, every single place you go? Plus, because my father stays by the car and never comes along to see these great sights, this adds considerably to my suspicion. If these landmarks are all so wondrous and important, why would he stay by the car and miss them?

I look at Lula for confirmation that this is true. Confirmation in general, I suppose. She nods. Maybe she's just humoring me, being nice, but I don't think so. She seems as if she really wants to hear what I have to say. She's patient, but seems like she's sort of on the edge of her seat at the same time. I take a deep breath and go on.

Way before we get to the Grand Canyon, I tell her, I'm pretty sure my mother is just making stuff up. By the time she is gesturing wildly while talking about time and a river and layers of rock and millions of years, millions and millions of years… I feel sad. Sad and confused. My neighbor Patsy already told me about the whole world being made in just seven short days, well six really, because God took one day off to rest, I guess. She learned this at her church, and this story is from God himself somehow. They said so at church, a Presbyterian one. But my other neighbor Carrie is an actual Catholic, and Carrie confirmed that this was, without question, the truth.

I feel a little better when my brother and I are allowed to feed some peanuts to the chipmunks that are running around everywhere. I am scared they will bite me, but they don't, and their teeny little claws feel creepy and good all at the same time when they crawl into my hand to get the nuts. I have to keep very, very still. If I do, they stay on my hand for a long time, and I feel like they are my personal friends.

We make one more stop, one last look at the immense canyon before the long slog home. My father doesn't even turn around to face it, just stands there in the doorway of the car with his back turned while he smokes. I look down at my bright, white saddle shoes. I look at Woo. He kicks his black Keds sneaker into the ground, sending up a fountain of dust. When the dust settles, we inch a little closer to the edge. There's no guardrail, no rope, no nothing. We can't believe it! We look at each other. We go closer. Woo kicks at the rocks and gravel at our feet again. Another cloud of dust soars into the air, but the bigger pebbles fly over the edge. We look at each other again. I pick up a handful of little rocks and hurl them as far as I can. We lean our heads out, peeking over the edge, when they begin their fall. Woo thrusts his foot forward so the tip of his shoe hangs off the edge. My eyes get big. I whip my head around and catch sight of my father. His crossed arms rest on the roof of the car, holding his cigarette. He wears the beige striped shirt with the little tiny hole pattern; it must be his favorite because he wears it lots of different days. His back faces us. In the other direction, my mother scrambles over some low rocks. The cord of her movie camera is tight around her wrist. Her other camera hangs from a strap around her neck. She needs to hold onto it so the camera won't bump against her and hurt her while she scrambles over the rocks to get some really good shots. She disappears around a corner. I can't see her anymore. Woo taunts me with his look. He cocks his head in a way that points his chin toward the edge. I watch for my mother to reappear, to come around the corner again. I try to move my eyes without moving my head, so Woo won't know how scared I am. I look at my father again. He has finished his cigarette and is sitting in the car. I think he's reading the map. He's looking down.

Woo moves his other foot. The toes of his other foot dangle now, too.

I inch my foot forward to do the same. Our toes, Woo's and mine, are hanging over the edge of the Grand Canyon. Woo covers his mouth with his hand and giggles. My mother calls for us to come on back to the car. I look over at her as she scrambles along a ledge. She's fussing with her camera. My parents didn't even see us playing right at the edge. Neither one of them. They never looked.

We drive away from the Grand Canyon, and there is a whirl going on inside of me. Kind of like when you make those paintings at carnivals, the ones where you squirt bright, beautiful colors from ketchup bottles, and then the whole thing spins around and you think it's going to be so so pretty—but it's a mess. An ugly, dark mess.

I am cranky and I stay that way the rest of the return trip, heading east once again on Route 66. Pancakes and motel swimming pools lose their allure, and hours upon hours bumping along in the back seat—with nothing supposedly dazzling to look forward to—are pure torture. After the mountains flatten out into the vast, monotonous, and scorching prairie, there aren't even any more roadside attractions to bring us to a halt. My mother packs away her movie camera one afternoon and the next day her regular camera and takes to staring silently out the window, turned away from all of us. My father stops pulling over to rest and smoke cigarettes; instead he lights up seemingly continually, sending endless clouds of choking smoke to add to our back-seat agonies.

My brother and I know that we are in big trouble if we fight or argue out loud, so we traverse a couple thousand miles of the United States by perpetuating a stealth war of silent punches, kicks, and the occasional pinch. It is the only entertainment we can muster.

When we get back home I am convinced that I am adopted, that I come from different people entirely than these two grown-ups who ping-pong between sphinxlike impenetrability and crazy, nonsensical laughter. I start to have scary dreams. In some of them, we are back on our road trip vacation. My parents leave me behind at one of the endless places where we stop. In others, I try as hard as I can to run away from something awful, but my legs don't work. It's as if I—my body—is winding down further and further into super-slow motion, while the rest of the world—and the scary threat—speed up and loom closer.

And then, I die. For the first time.

It's so hot and so dry. The sky is a burning blaze of white. No wind. The air is so still that it's completely silent. It's like being in a movie theater when the sound snaps off, and the picture continues. I think I must have suddenly gone deaf, and I look around to see if anything is moving—a branch, a lizard, a bird —something I should be able to hear.

There is young woman in front of me. She wears traditional native dress. A skirt that goes all the way to the ground, a long-sleeve shirt with the cuffs rolled up to reveal inches and inches of bracelets. She has a single, waist-length braid that's bound with a thin leather strap. She turns briefly when I approach the edge and then looks back down. She doesn't say a word. She doesn't say hello, which I think is odd, because almost everyone says hello to a four-year-old child, especially one who is approaching the edge of the Grand Canyon.

She sits very near the edge herself. But she's not actually sitting. I realize that she's crouched, and she stays like that as if it's the most relaxed position in the world. She is weaving a basket. I watch the quickness of her hands, young hands, and I think she might be very young despite the baby beside her. A papoose. I am proud of myself for knowing the word for a Native American baby who's all bound up in a beautiful little cocoon. The baby is wide-awake, but utterly silent, his calm black eyes staring far into the distance.

I think that both of them must be miserably hot. In my 1960 shorts and sleeveless blouse, I can't imagine how they seem so—

My foot slips. My saddle shoe's heel scrapes against the parched dirt. It's so slow at first, just a grating of my calf. I feel the skin rub away, then the first tiny droplets of blood rising to the surface. Then time speeds up. My feet fly out from under me. I am face-to-face with the white-hot sky. I am in free fall. Falling. Falling.

My back hits first. The sensation, the pain I suppose I would call it, lasts for a mere second. It's like the wind being knocked out of me, except I know that it's not the wind. I am surrounded by the blackest, darkest night, but within the black, an ocean of spark-like bursts of light fly from my body in all directions at once. I die.

I am dead.

I am gasping for breath I am trying to reach the surface I am trying to keep my lungs from bursting I am straining to see something besides the sparks inky black nothing and the sparks and I gasp and I cough and I sputter and an arm is on me…no two arms are on me. They're around me and it's Lula and she's with me and I hear words; she's saying words to me. She is saying, "You are right here, Mazie. You are right here."

I say her name: "Lula." I say it over and over. I keep saying it until I once again recognize the sound of my own voice. Until I am no longer in the dark bedroom of my childhood. Sparks no longer fly from my little body. The eternal battleship gray of the farm's porch floor comes into focus. Songs of birds reach into my ears and shatter the silence of my death.

Lula holds her hands on my upper arms. She holds me tight. A shudder runs the length of my body and leaves me trembling. I can't stop trembling. My lip quivers as I look into Lula's eyes and say, "What just happened? What in the world just happened to me?"

"You were telling me about your dream," she says. "It must have been very powerful, especially for such a young child."

"No, Lula," I say. "I was *there*. It wasn't remembering. I was back there. I felt the exact same things that I felt at the time. The same as when I had the dream in the first place. The sensations. The sparks of light. All of it." My breathing becomes ragged and uneven again. I feel as if I may start gasping for air any second.

Lula runs a gentle hand down the length of my hair and brushes my cheek with her fingers. My body lets out a sigh. I inhale a great breath, feeling the mountain air flooding into my lungs. Lula says, "Your memories are vivid, indeed, dear. Vivid indeed." She squeezes my hand and holds it.

I begin to feel like I am being very silly, *indeed,* to use Lula's wonderful word. Of course I was just remembering. Of course. What in the world else could it be? I stand behind the chair that had always been my mother's. I run my hands along the welted seam of the—what was it called…Naugahyde?—chair, the miracle synthetic material that supposedly lasts forever. I scan the gray, marble-patterned Formica table. My parents would be pleased to know that the chairs and table they chose so carefully with their ceaseless devotion to thrift and endurance—things that would stand up to children, animals, friends, and the vicissitudes of life in general with a minimum of worry or bother—had indeed withstood the test of time.

An awkward giggle involuntarily escapes from my mouth, a sign of my immense embarrassment. Lula smiles at me but says nothing.

"You must think I was the strangest child," I say to Lula. "Well, I told you I was. Now you can see for yourself."

"Not so far, dear. Not so far."

"I guess we should deal a hand?" I ask. "I'm not really sure what to do."

"Seems to me just the sort of time that card playing was invented for," Lula says.

"For times when someone has just re-experienced her own death?" I say. Lula knows that I'm being neither mocking nor acerbic. She knows that I'm being playful. I am feeling good.

I know she knows because she says, "Yes, exactly," with a completely straight face while arranging her cards.

...8

It seems like the same day, but it isn't. The sun set and rose again; at least I am pretty sure that happened. The days blur together. Lula and I sit at our places on the porch. She arranges her cards. She drinks her entire glass of ice water in two gulps. I fetch her a fresh glass while she arranges her cards again. Everything feels profoundly familiar. And utterly unknown.

Lula takes her turn and says, "Do you mind if I ask you a question, dear? About what we were discussing the other day?"

"No," I say, "I guess not. But I do notice that I do *all* the talking. And when you do talk, you usually talk *about me*. I don't know much about you, Lula. I'd like to! I understand that this is largely my doing. I've certainly noted my own rambling tendencies, which you definitely bring out in me. Which sounds like I'm somehow blaming you. Which I'm not. There's something about the way you are that makes me want to talk—not just talk, but…open up. Like, for instance, how my attempt to get you to talk more, which is what I've been trying to do right now, has already gotten derailed into yet another soliloquy."

"I love your stories," Lula says. "They fill you up and flow forth like they're a part of the landscape, as if they circle around us and settle to the ground and stay."

"I have no idea what you just said," I say. "But…circle around us…a part of the landscape…what a lovely idea. Really. Still, I'd like to know about *you*."

"May I ask my question first?" Lula says.

I say sure, and she says, "The dream that you were telling me about. That particular dream—it was so frightening. You must have been so scared, so confused. Especially since you were very young." Lula puts down her cards and reaches across the table to rest her hand on top of mine. "Did you tell anyone about it?"

I let out a small chuckle and say, "No. No way." I think for a moment and add, "I might have gone into my parents' room. I used to do that when I was still little. If I was particularly scared about something, I would get up and wander into their bedroom and crawl under the covers beside my mother. I was allowed to do this if I didn't awaken them and didn't move around. I had to force myself to lie as still as I could. Then I could stay for a while. I used to watch the little patterns and swirls that your eyeballs see sometimes when it's dark and still. They were strangely comforting; in fact, I would crawl into their bed and wait for the patterns to show up. After a while my mother would stir and say, 'OK, Mazie, that's long enough. Go back to your own room now.' But that was OK, really. My parents' bed smelled strongly of the two of them, all intermingled together, and between the smell and their heavy breathing and the little floating dots, I felt OK again."

"I'm amazed that such a young child wouldn't tell anyone about something so frightening," Lula says.

"Really?" I ask her. "Is that so unusual?"

"I hardly consider myself the expert on 'usual,' but it would seem so to me."

"I never really thought about it. About telling anyone, I mean." I look through the screen and focus on the tall spruce between us and the orchard. I shift my eyes to the orchard beyond, then snap them back to look at Lula. "I guess I haven't really told you what a scared little kid I was." I take a deep breath. "I know I've told you some, but…I haven't been entirely honest. I really thought I was crazy." I take another long breath and a tall drink from my own glass of ice water. "There. I've said it. My deep, dark secret. I figured it out quite early. To stop telling people things that I was thinking. The things that would get that…reaction. The reaction that told me I was the scared, nutty kid I thought I was. A kid who saw danger everywhere."

I feel my cheeks flush. The tops of my ears feel like they have burst into flames.

Lula has kindness in her eyes. Nothing but kindness. I'm pretty sure.

I say, "Do you know what telling you that dream made *me* think of? It reminded me of the time that same aunt and uncle and—by then—three cousins came from California to visit us, and the whole kit and caboodle came to our farm.

Three little girls. After my aunt lost all those babies—fifteen, I was told—she had three in a row, bang bang bang, all girls. First a blonde with piercing gray eyes and an old-soul seriousness. Once I got over my initial inexperience with babies in general, and my cousin in particular, I thought she was fascinating. Next came a dark brunette, with huge brown eyes and round red cheeks who grinned ear-to-ear at everything. Another blonde arrived third, but not the white blonde of her oldest sister. This one's hair looked as if it had been painted by hand, the streaks of varying yellow tones perfectly drawn. She sucked her middle two fingers, not her thumb, which I thought was the most adorable, heart-melting, and wildly exotic thing imaginable. I watched her in her highchair, the sun doing magic with the bands of color in her hair, as she sucked her tiny fingers in between bites of food.

They were like fairies to me. Perfect little creatures from some other world where they had their own secret language and habits and riddles.

On one of their visits to our old farm, when they were around four, five, and six years old, the cloudless summer sky suddenly changed hue to a slight gray. In less than an hour, the sky was a solid ceiling of deep steel. You could no longer see individual clouds; it felt rather that the sky had moved closer to the earth and was threatening to crush it.

At first, I wasn't sure if what I was seeing was a muted flash, a suggestion of light through the thick wall of clouds. The faint rumble a number of seconds later affirmed that it was.

My little cousins had never seen a thunderstorm. There was no such thing where they came from. And though they had heard about the storms and read about them in books, they could no more imagine the reality than I could understand their secret language.

After the first low growl of thunder, my aunt gathered her daughters. They stood on the porch of our farm, waiting. The first few raindrops plopped, slowly enough that you could hear each one hit the leaf or branch or patch of ground where it landed. The rain turned into a gentle, steady shower, and a more distinct flash of light lit the cloud cover. I don't know which of the little cousins let out the first scream when the thunder came, but they all followed suit. The shower became a downpour, a rain unlike any they had seen. The girls grabbed one another's hands and stood in a tight circle.

A bolt of lightning shot through the air at the edge of the orchard, fifty yards or so from where we all stood, close enough that we heard the sizzle as the massive electricity seared through the air. The quickly following clap of thunder was deafening, but not so loud that it drowned out the little girls. They screamed in terror and laughed with delight and clutched tight to each other's hands and danced and jumped and screamed some more.

The next lightning bolt came right on the heels of the last and was even closer. We saw it stab into a high branch on one of the tallest trees at the orchard's edge. The branch crashed to the ground, the sound completely obliterated by the roar of the thunder. The porch shook beneath our feet. I had never felt the ground beneath my feet move before, and I could not fathom how this could happen. But my cousins had grown up where there are earthquakes and did not bat an eye.

It was a day of magic. Of the once-solid earth moving beneath me. Of electric bolts lighting up the sky. Of the air around us dividing in two and crashing back together in an earsplitting roar. The little cousins. The Weird Sisters. The Three Fates.

The kind of magic that has always been here.

The towering thunderstorm swept through and beyond us with the same swiftness that marked its arrival. The sky faded back to a lighter gray for a short while. With no apparent transition whatsoever, the sun suddenly blazed in a completely cloudless afternoon sky. When the sun's hot tendrils found their way to the water that covered every surface of the lush forest, when the tendrils wormed their way into the sodden earth, an upsurge of swamp-like muggy air rose from the ground. We were in a virtual hothouse, an atmosphere so overripe and fecund that it felt primeval.

The adults became woozy and slow. The cousins were droopy but restless after the exhilaration of the storm. We decided to venture outside and see if walking through the tall, drenched meadow grass would cool us.

Woo led our pack, followed by the cousins, with me bringing

up the rear. My shoes and socks were instantly soaked. I ran my hands along the Queen Anne's lace and the feathery tops of the field grasses, letting the water droplets drench my shirt.

Mid-stride, I pivoted on my foot and broke into a run back toward the house. Tears streamed down my cheeks. A ferocious pain shot from my ankle and worsened by the second. I could not even speak by the time I got back to the house, but managed to hobble and point to the spot, which my mother immediately recognized as a bee sting. She sat me down at the porch table and went to the kitchen to mix a potion of baking soda and water. Just as she was dabbing it on my bee sting, shrieks of screaming and crying rose from the meadow. The grown-ups leaped into action and met a hysterical group of three sobbing girls, plus my brother Woo doing an impressive job of appearing stoic even while he winced in pain.

I had apparently been stung by a lone rogue, but my brother and the cousins had stepped on the ground wasps' actual nest while crossing the meadow. The adults went into triage mode, checking each child to count sting marks and assess general damage. The middle cousin had not been stung. Her cries had emanated from the interconnected webbing of sisterhood. Woo and the oldest cousin had three stings each. The littlest cousin had taken the biggest hit by far. My aunt didn't bother to count. She scooped her baby up in her arms and plopped down in a chair and pulled her in close close close. She rocked and sang to her. She patted her beautiful striped hair and moved little strands of it from her face. She stroked her cheek. The littlest cousin sobbed for a long time, her chest heaving violently every so often. But my aunt held her tight and whispered to her, their faces practically touching, their breaths mingling. I could see the little cousin's gangly legs begin to relax, her foot loosening first. The calm climbed up her calf and past her knee. After a long time, her whole leg swung easily back and forth as my aunt rocked.

My mother stood in the doorway between the kitchen and the porch. She watched over the scene from a distance. She unfolded her arms from across her chest as she said, 'Want some more iced tea, Marilyn?' But my aunt didn't hear her. She cooed and stroked. She saw nothing but her wounded baby who needed her.

I remain in a dreamy nostalgic reverie for a few seconds after I finish that last sentence, then burst into a full belly laugh. "Well, so much for our first day hearing more about your life," I say to Lula. "And so much for good intentions. I do believe that is my longest story so far. By about a mile."

...9

"**Y**ou're very different than my great-aunt Lula," I say, noting Lula's worn brown hiking trousers. She has rolled the cuffs to expose a few inches of her translucent pale ankles sticking into her socks, which are ever-so-slightly different shades of off-white. I want to hug her or cry or something; she seems so utterly and perfectly herself. "I think Aunt Lula wore a double strand of pearls every day of her life. The big ones, marble-sized, almost. Not exactly the outdoorsy type."

"I suppose that wasn't very common back then," Lula suggests. "Being the 'outdoorsy type.' Especially if she was a city gal."

"City gal. I like that," I say. "Are we playing seven cards or ten today, by the way?"

"Let's play ten, if you're amenable."

"I only knew Great-Aunt Lula at the very end of her life. She was living with her youngest sister in a house that seemed enormous to me. The youngest and the oldest of five sisters living together, both long widowed. My mother would take my brother and me to visit. By then, Aunt Lula was confined to one upstairs room. She couldn't climb stairs any longer. When we first started visiting her, Aunt Lula would be sitting in a chair in her room, reading a book. Wearing a dress—not a housedress, like my other grandmother and her sisters wore, but a dress that was much fancier. Solid color, wool, tailored. Her hair was completely white. She was the oldest person I had ever seen, and I thought every single thing about her was fascinating. And she scared me, too. But like I told you, I was scared of pretty much everything.

"After a while, Aunt Lula was bedridden. No more chair. No more books, either. When we'd come to visit, she'd be sitting up in bed, wearing an elaborate nightgown and a bed jacket, and still the pearls! But just sitting or lying there. She always had a little smile on her face, even before she knew we were there. I really do think she was happy. Living out her life in that bed. Her baby sister keeping her company, bringing her food and anything she needed.

"We had to sit right on the bed, so she could hear us. My mother would sit on one side of her, and my brother and I would take turns sitting next to her arm, on the other side of her. My mother's family weren't the warm, huggy types. I had never been that close to her—physically close—while she was still able to sit in a chair. I couldn't believe the whiteness of her hair, all of it in wonderful loose curls that covered her head. Did you ever hear it said that our strongest and longest memories are of smell, Lula? I still remember exactly the way that Great-Aunt Lula smelled—a combination of something very faint and girly, like dusting powder maybe. Dusting powder was a popular thing back then; I used to buy it for my mother for every single holiday. A tinge of the unmistakable smell of Listerine—the original one, the amber one that tasted awful and medicinal and bitter and like of course it would kill every single germ in your mouth or anywhere else. And the smell that was *her*, the completely unique scent that was hers and hers alone. All those things were mixed together. And laundry detergent. The detergent that her nightgowns and sheets and pillowcases and bed jackets had all been washed with. That was Aunt Lula."

"Did you just sniff me, dear?" Lula asks me.

"What? Did I?" I am sure that I'm already beet red. "Gosh, I'm sorry. Old habit. Memory. I always drank in her scent. I think I might have been more subtle about it back then. When I was six."

I am mortified. I look deeply into Lula's face, checking for any of the signs—the signs that used to tell me that I was, indeed, odd. Lula's face is relaxed. Her eyebrows are very slightly raised in an expression that conveys interest. Curiosity. Waiting for more.

113

"The strangest thing happened the last time we visited her," I continue. "Strange considering that, really, I hardly knew Aunt Lula. She had moved in with her sister not that long before she died. Before that, she lived in Washington, D.C., and I'd never even met her. I would guess we didn't visit her more than four or five times total before she died.

"It was my turn to sit next to her on the bed. She reached over for my hand, and she picked it up and held it. It was the first time I had ever felt her skin. I'm not sure I can even describe it. It felt as thin and dry and fragile as an old piece of newspaper, but tough at the same time. Strong. The veins stood out so bright blue on the back of her hand, her skin looked nearly transparent. I thought if I looked hard enough, I'd be able to see the blood moving through those veins, heading back up to her heart. And her touch was so light, I wasn't even sure if she was still holding my hand when she said, 'I had a dream about you the other night. You and I were walking up a hillside, a beautiful, grassy hillside. Just you and me. Isn't that the funniest thing, Mazie?'

"And I thought: 'Yes, Aunt Lula, yes that is the funniest thing. You hardly know me. You have your own children and grandchildren and a million nieces and nephews and great nieces and great nephews. And I'm the one in your dream. Walking over a hillside.'

"I was terrified. I was sure it must mean something awful would happen," I say. "But you know what? I couldn't get that picture out of my mind, of Great-Aunt Lula and me walking over a hillside together. It gave me the most peaceful feeling, like that was a place I wanted to be. Like this farm is for me: a place I just need to come to sometimes."

"Mazie, you certainly seem to have a thing or two that you want to say," Lula says.

"Oh, geez Lula, I'm sorry. I'm talking your ear off. Again. No, no. I've yak-yakked you nearly to death. Again," I say. "I'm truly sorry. Not to mention embarrassed."

"When I come back tomorrow," Lula says, "I will look forward to hearing more. And perhaps we'll even play some cards."

"You have a dry sort of humor, Lula. Do you know that?" I say.

Lula smiles, closes the porch door behind her, and starts up the path toward the road.

I'm ready, Lula thought. She looked down at her hands, resting on top of the thick blanket. They no longer looked like hands to her. In the craggy blue veins, she saw the branches of ancient, sturdy trees lifting to the sky. She saw their deep, formidable roots, reaching down, down into the earth. She saw water flowing through creeks and streams and rivers.

I am ready to go. There is one more thing I must do. Mazie will come to visit. She will sit next to me on this bed. I will touch her hand. I will tell her that I dreamed of her. She will be frightened, but she will always remember. She will remember the feeling, the peacefulness, the comfort. Far from here, she will meet another old woman with my same name. She needs to trust Lula. She must.

... 10

I wait at the porch door, standing on my tiptoes and watching for Lula to come through the orchard at her usual time. When she is close enough to hear me, I call out, "Lula, do you know what I just realized? It's blueberry time! It should be just about peak blueberry-picking right now! You probably haven't even seen them. They grow along the bank on the far side of the road—the stretch of road that runs right along the length of the orchard! See what I mean? If you're walking through the orchard itself, you'd never even know the bushes were there!"

Lula turns her body around. "Ah, right as rain, Mazie. Sure enough, I've never seen a single bush."

"That's because the road at the far end of the orchard—where you come in over yonder—it's deep in the shade of the woods. The orchard opens everything up. A little patch of sun hits the bank, and *Voila!* Wild blueberries!" Even in the midst of my excitement, I notice how heavily Lula leans on her walking stick. "Are you tired, Lula? Do you want to rest up with a tall glass of water? I was thinking I might go and pick some of the berries. Was thinking that I would whip up some blueberry pancakes for us. Have us a true hearty breakfast, if you're game."

"My word, that does sound lovely," Lula says.

"You can wait here, if you want. I'm happy to go and pick them. If you want to sit a spell."

"Oh, heavens no. Not so tired that I can't pick a blueberry off a bush. Not to mention, can't trust a weekender to tell a truly good, ripe berry from a bad one," Lula says.

"Oh, ouch," I say. "I was wondering how long it would take you to bring up the weekender thing, me being an interloper and not true country and all that."

"Well, I didn't mean to hurt your feelings. Just meant to say that of course I want to come along," Lula says. "Assuming you have a proper berry-picking bucket, that is."

I sigh dramatically and do an exaggerated eye roll. "Gosh, let me go look. You stay here and rest; don't strain yourself trying to think up any more witty things to say." I rummage around in the kitchen and manage to find the two old enamel berry pails that my family used. I set them on the kitchen floor beside me and gaze at them and smile. I treat them as if they are long-lost, dear friends whose very presence I cannot get enough of.

I can't wait to show them to Lula. But when I see her sitting on the porch, with what my husband Eddie would call a "thousand-yard stare," I still think she looks weary, and I decide to keep my blueberry pail excitement to myself. I don't want to hurt her feelings by asking her a second time if she wants to come with me, but I don't want to be insensitive if she really is too tired. Maybe she doesn't want to hurt *my* feelings. I muster my breeziest voice to assure her it won't take me very long to pick a few berries and that she sure looks mighty comfortable. She dismisses me with a wave of her hand, so I walk over and hold the porch door for her to follow. "If you go through the orchard, it's a hazardous rocky mess; if we go up the path, it's steep. Let me take your arm, Lula," I say.

She jerks her arm away from my reach. I'm gobsmacked. My mouth falls open. "Sorry to startle you, dear. I actually do better on my own. It's easier to keep a steady balance with just my own movements to worry about."

"Oh, ok," I say, but I feel hurt. Unreasonably so, even though I understand I'm being tetchy and petty. Lula senses this from me, and I sense that Lula senses it. The two of us are quiet as we make our way up the path and down the road to the blueberry bushes. This has all gotten senselessly complicated, or at least I hope that's the case. I hope it can be brought back to the ease, the effortless, straightforward comfort I so often feel in Lula's presence.

"Do you have any idea why some blueberries have that white coating on them and others don't? Should I stay away from the whitish ones?" I ask.

"I do know!" Lula says. "That white coating is called the 'bloom.' It's a slightly waxy substance that the berry produces; the bloom protects it from pests and bacteria that might harm the berry. Isn't that amazing?" Lula's delight radiates from her. "It's also a sign of freshness. It's the *other* blueberries that we should stay away from. The berries start out with the bloom when they're beautifully ripe, but it fades as they sit on the bush past their prime."

"Do you know everything, Lula? 'Cause it's really starting to seem like you know everything."

"Heavens no, dear," Lula says. "But like I told you, I know a lot about things from around here. I've always been here, like I said!"

"What's the tenth decimal place of pi?" I randomly ask.

"Five," Lula says.

Both of us stop picking and turn to look at one another. When she sees the surprise—well, alarm, really—on my face, she bursts out laughing. And I do, too. "Well, I've studied a few other things along the way, I suppose," Lula says. She spreads her arms and shrugs her shoulders in that distinctive Lula way. "My bucket is getting pretty full, Mazie. How about yours?"

I lean down to look into my bucket. I feel something strike my cheek, and I instinctively swat at it, as if it were a gnat or a mosquito. When I see a lone blueberry hit the ground by my foot, I swing around to look at Lula. She is leaning against the bank at the side of the road, her blueberry bucket on the ground by her feet and her hands folded in her lap.

"That was weird," I say.

"What was, dear?"

"I think that a blueberry just hit me on the cheek." I scan her features keenly.

"On the cheek? It's not as if they can fly, Mazie." Lula ponders for a minute. "I suppose a bird could have dropped one, though. That might explain it."

"A bird," I say. I look around the woods, then up at the sky. While I'm looking up, another blueberry hits me squarely on the chin. I whip around to find Lula leaning peacefully, the bucket still on the ground and her hands still folded.

"Are you throwing blueberries at me, Lula?" I ask her.

"Ha!" Lula laughs. "Am I *what*?"

"Well, a berry just hit me on the chin! I don't understand how this could be happening." I stand still for a moment and do my best to look thoughtful. I feign turning my head away from Lula, then snap it back in the other direction to find Lula holding a single berry in her hand, ready to throw it. "Oh my God, how old are you?" I say. "You seriously had me thinking that I was going nuts. Too much time alone in the woods or something."

Lula stares at her shoes and looks a bit sheepish. "Gotta say though," I tell her, "your aim is really good. Impressive for such a *very old* person."

"Touché," Lula says. "Indeed, touché."

I look off into the distance, for real this time. "Where are we, Lula?" I say.

"Not sure I get your meaning, dear." Lula stoops to pick up her berry bucket.

"I'm not sure what I mean either," I say. "I was thinking about the paint on the porch floor. When we were playing cards the other day. I was thinking about how perfect it looked. Like it had just been painted yesterday. Not a sign of wear. Not a scuff or a mark or a…clump of dirt."

"Can't say as I ever thought about it," Lula says.

"And the blueberries. Look how many we picked just now. Look how many berries are still on the bushes. I don't ever remember a crop like this one," I say.

"Isn't nature a marvel?" Lula says. "So many different ingredients—temperature and sun and rainfall and time—it's different every year. This is a banner summer for blueberries, that's for sure."

"Everything seems a little weirdly perfect this summer," I say.

Lula reaches out and puts her hand on my arm, "At this point in my long life, who am I to argue with perfection?"

I glance down at Lula's hand then meet her gaze. "What was I saying? I feel like I lose my train of thought all the time lately." I pick up my berry bucket and say, "I suppose that's more than enough berries for the two of us. Let's head on back to the house."

We walk in silence down the dirt road. I close my eyes and turn my face toward the last bright beam of sun before we enter the shade. I can feel the smile spread across my face. I am thinking about Eddie.

"Did I ever tell you about my husband Eddie? Well, that's a ridiculous question. I just met you; of course, I never told you about him. I was so scared to bring him here the first time, Lula. So scared that he wouldn't *get it*, you know? Don't think I

121

was ever so nervous in all my life as when we hit the top of the dirt road up there," I point in the direction Lula walks when she leaves. "That road terrifies lots of people. Especially if they grew up in the city, like he did. Especially if they've never seen a dirt road with hogback ridges like ours, not to mention steep banks on either side. Most people are panicked way before they have to drive right through the creek down yonder. Anyway, we made the turn from the gravel road onto Noel Road up there and...I'll never forget Eddie's face. He turned his head from side to side, and his mouth dropped open. And he let out a whoop, an honest-to-god whoop, and he said, "We need a car with a sunroof, baby; I need to see all of this at once. All of it!" And he let out another whoop, and I laughed. And all the nerves in my whole body calmed right down. Eddie. I called him, 'Eddie, my Eddie.'"

"It's good to hear you laugh, Mazie," Lula says. "Really good. You never laughed enough."

I wipe a tear from my eye and chuckle a couple of times before Lula's statement fully registers. "Wait. What did you say? I 'never laughed enough' when?"

"Hmm? Oh, did I say that? I suppose I meant that I haven't heard you laugh very much. Since I've known you," Lula says.

"But you said, I 'never *laughed* enough.' Past tense. Like you're talking about some time...or something...that's gone."

"I misspoke, I guess," Lula says, spreading her arms and shrugging in that way she has. "You're the one who keeps reminding me how terribly ancient I am. Now you're making an old gal feel bad. I misspoke is all."

"If you say so. You're creeping me out a little, is all," I say.

"'Creeping me out,'" Lula says. "What on earth does that mean?"

"It means you're weirding me out!"

"Well, that certainly clears it up," Lula says. We have reached the porch's screen door, which Lula lets slam behind her. She sets her berry bucket on the table and begins to pull out her chair to sit, but then she pauses. "Actually, let's walk a little more," she says. "Let's work up a wee tad more appetite for those pancakes."

That's funny. I never heard anyone else say "wee tad" before except me. I guess I thought I made it up, but I couldn't have if Lula knows the expression, too. When she steps off the porch again, Lula begins walking the short distance toward the orchard. I follow along for a few steps then stop. "I don't want to go that way," I say. I feel sick. My stomach clenches. My head feels woozy. I feel like I need to work hard to breathe.

"I think we can go this way, dear," Lula says. "I think we can."

I take just a few more steps and stop at the post-and-rail fence that marks the edge of the orchard. "I feel really bad, Lula. I think I need to go back to the house and sit down for a bit."

"I think a little more air may do you some good, Mazie. How about if we walk this way then?" Lula asks me as she starts down the path in front of the house.

The nausea seems to be passing. I feel better. "Oh, no, you're heading straight for the old outhouse," I even try to joke. "Is that your idea of getting some air? A tour of the old outhouse?"

"Not the outhouse," Lula laughs. "We'll go past it, then, over that way," she says, raising her walking stick into the air to point.

"The creek is over that way," I say. "You can't see it, but it's around that bend up there and down a ways. Good idea; I'd like to check how it's running this summer. It might even be dried up already. I usually check it every day when I'm here. I can't believe I haven't walked out to it yet—another one of those things that keeps slipping my mind, I guess. It's one of those things I count on—checking it every single day. Because every single day there are changes. How the water pours over the rocks at the top of the little waterfall. How the stream breaks into rivulets on its way across the mossy rocks. How the moss grows thick enough that chunks break off and float away. How the burbles and waves at the waterfall's base swell and shrink and move." I stop and look at Lula. I'm not embarrassed even though tears are welling in my eyes. "It's amazing, Lula. How different every single day is from every other. I used to spend hours studying that creek. *Hours.*"

"Miracles abound for those who notice," Lula says.

"Pithy! Did you just make that up?" We are both light. Buoyant, even.

"Probably," Lula says. "Although I may have heard it somewhere and am just too old to remember." She inhales a great breath and exhales audibly, "You go on up ahead and get reacquainted with your creek. I'll toddle along and find my way to meet you."

I look up the path and then look Lula up and down. "We came out here because *you* thought that *I* needed a little air.

Are you doing OK? I am more than happy to go back and sit on the porch. We can swing on the porch swing!"

"I am absolutely fine, dear. Just want to take my time. Now, shoo. Shoo, shoo. Go check your creek." She gives my back a firm pat of encouragement, then an affectionate push.

I can't believe I haven't checked the creek yet. I trot the remaining distance across the field; round the corner past the dense stand of tangled, overgrown raspberry bushes; and into the patch of deep woods that leads to the creek. When I spot it, I can't believe it! I have never seen the creek running this full at this point in the summer—a gentle, steady stream! There's enough water to create a quiet murmur of ripples as the creek makes its way down the waterfall's short drop and across the jumble of rocks at the base. The small stones that traverse the creek—which remain completely underwater until late spring —show a clear path across the water. I leap across the whole span, touching only one stone on my crossing. I pivot on the far bank and reach my arms out for balance. I want to cross back to my starting point by balancing on each individual rock for as long as I can. When I am just about midway across, I see something that may be a baby salamander skittering out from beneath a rock on the creek bottom. I gasp out loud and, without thinking, dive into the water on my hands and knees to get a better look.

Fiery, sharp stabs shoot from the bottoms of my feet straight into my brain. There is ice in the creek; there is snow all around me. I just stand there. I stand there with my feet in the creek until I am sure that in one more second my legs will buckle underneath me; they will no longer be able to hold my weight. In one more second, I will not be able to get out of the creek, will not be able to run back to the house. I sob from the pain, my breath coming in great frozen gasps.

I make a dive for the bank of the creek and lay face down in the snow, my frozen legs and feet waving in the air toward the winter sky.

I roll onto my back and am blinded by the intense brightness of the sun. I hold a hand in front of my face to block it out. An aura appears around it, like my hand has its own halo. My other arm reaches out beside me, and I feel damp, packed dirt at the creek's edge. The roar of the creek recedes into a gentle burble. The steely winter sky transforms into a deep, cloudless blue. I turn my head from side to side, expecting to see deep drifts of snow. They are gone. The whole world is green and alive.

I sit up. Lula sits beside me on the bank. Her knee leans against mine.

My clothes—my shoes and the bottoms of my pants—are completely soaked. I'm a bit muddled. I try to piece it together but can't. It's like a dream that you remember in vivid detail when you first awaken, only to find that every bit of the dream has vanished just a short time later. I kick my soggy shoe out toward Lula and say, "I thought I saw a salamander or a newt. I was trying to get a closer look."

... II

I blow across the top of my coffee and watch the vapor waft away into the summer morning. Lula shuffles the ancient deck of cards. The cards' edges are minutely blacker each morning. Their corners bend down like dog-eared bookmarks. Lula and I leave traces on them, a little more of ourselves each day. We add our own skin cells and oil and dirt from our fingers to all the human remnants that came before us.

"I was thinking about time," I say to her. "Well, I guess it's more accurate to say timing. The timing of things. I could be a night owl. I might lay awake for hours at night staring at the ceiling, unable to sleep, crippled by insomnia. I might wander through the house or do crossword puzzles or compose poems in a secret notebook that I would hide under the mattress. I would wait, pray, and become desperate for the ever-evasive sleep. Which, when it finally came, would send me into a blessed nothingness that kept me in bed until noon." I smile at Lula. "If I weren't a morning person, I never would have met you. Never would have had a hint that you even *existed*. I wouldn't be awake when you take your morning walks. And you wouldn't have known that I existed either. We would not have crossed paths. You would have taken your walks and seen an empty old farmhouse porch in front of you every day. I would have come out to the porch with my coffee—even if it were just moments later—and I would never have seen a soul walking across the orchard."

"I suppose that's true," Lula says.

"Timing was strangely at work in the way that I met Eddie, too." I want to talk about Eddie. I want to be with him, have him here with me. I want Lula to know him. "I actually met him a year before I really met him. I know that doesn't make any sense, but I'll explain. We went out on a couple of dates late one summer. I thought he was OK. Cute, with one dimple when he smiled—I'm a sucker for that. But all in all…just OK. I was pretty sure he felt the same way about me. Interested— well, at least in a sexual sense. His eyes kept wandering down toward my breasts most of the way through our second date —but maybe not all that interested otherwise. He went out of town for a couple of weeks right after the second date, and my interest just…fizzled. Eddie called eventually—after he got back to town—but I told him I'd gotten interested in someone else, which wasn't even true, and that was the end of that.

"Strangely enough, almost exactly one year later, I found myself thinking about him. I had this feeling that I should… get in touch with him. I hadn't kept his phone number, so the only option I could think of was to call him at his work and leave a message. I gathered up my courage, and I called. I left him a voice message and asked if he had any interest in catching up, and I left my number. He called back that same day and left a message for me saying that he *would* like to catch up. Something in his voice sounded almost as if he'd been waiting all that time for my call. Surprised, but not surprised. Then he called and left a second message, because he was worried that his first message might seem…unenthusiastic. The new message said that he'd been in a bike accident and had broken his leg. He was hobbling around on crutches and still in a lot of pain. He said if he had sounded odd or lukewarm it was strictly because he was worn out by the broken leg. The accident had been only about three weeks before I called.

"I called him in person to tell him how sorry I was about the leg, and I told him I thought we should wait to get together until he was feeling better. He didn't want to wait. He wanted to set up something as soon as we could. He suggested meeting for coffee the coming weekend.

"When I walked into the café he'd picked out, he was seated at the bar. It was the end of August, and the late summer sun was shining on his left arm, lighting up the metal rim around his watch and all of the little golden hairs on his arm. A thrill ran through me—his watch, the golden hairs, the way his arm rested on top of the bar. He was turned away from where I'd come in, and he reached that arm out to adjust the crutches next to him, tenderly, almost as if they were his companions. He looked back in my direction, and his face lit up into this... beautiful smile.

"I have no idea what we talked about. Does anyone remember those kinds of things?

"The hours went by. The light pouring in through the front windows changed continually. I ran my finger along the glossy varnished wood of the beautiful old bar. We switched from coffee to wine. We got hungry and ordered food, and then we ordered more wine. The bartender polished glass after glass, trying as hard as he could to be subtle while he witnessed the unfolding that was happening between Eddie and me.

"I remember when Eddie reached over and touched my arm while making a point. I remember when my fingertips drifted down from the bar and grazed his thigh.

"He looked at me, bold and shy all at once. Fierce and tentative. The thought came into my head like a shock of lightning: my future. This man could be my future. Mid-sentence, mid-sip, mid-everything, I leaned over and kissed him. Not a peck, a real kiss. A real one. And then I kissed him again."

"That's lovely, just lovely," Lula says. I feel like I should make her some popcorn. She is hanging on my every word. Her eyes are saucer large.

I feel so light, like my body has no weight to it. I laugh; I hear the complete lack of strain, of anything but buoyancy in my own laugh. "Later, Eddie told me that one of his good friends lived in the same neighborhood that I did. He said the two of them got together every couple of weeks and that every time they had gotten together for the past year, Eddie had thought of me. Every time. He didn't know exactly where I lived, but he knew generally. He said he would picture me, in an apartment he had never actually seen, wearing clothes he'd never seen me wear, going about my life. For a whole year.

"And then I called.

"Timing. Like I said.

"Why were we both so…halfhearted the first time around? And a year later: magic.

"If I get started talking about Eddie, we're likely to be here all day," I say.

Lula smiles. I melt right into that smile like a chocolate bar in the sun.

"We got married here, Eddie and I." Lula puts her cards down, and I laugh. "Let me get us some more water, and I'll tell you about it. *If* you'd like. Really, Lula, it's up to you. Nothing *I'd* rather do than talk about marrying Eddie, but…"

"Not sure I can imagine a much better use of a beautiful summer day," she says.

When I come back from the kitchen with our water, I bring the two remaining stems of jewelweed that Lula brought a week ago. I had taken them into the kitchen to throw them away—the rest of the flowers had long died—but I couldn't bear to throw out the very last ones. I put them on the table, right where they sat in their vase when they were in their fresh, glorious peak.

I always wanted to get married at the farm. From the very first summer after we bought it. When the wildflowers and the mountain laurels burst out that first spring, and the ferns came out of nowhere with their fragile, curled fiddleheads pushing through the still-cold ground and stretching toward the sky. This is the place, I thought, where I want to join another person's life. I will gather an armful of wildflowers as I walk to meet my future husband. The orange of lilies, the creamy white of Queen Anne's lace, the vibrant gold of black-eyed Susans, the lavender of wild phlox. Maybe I would weave a crown of flowers to wear around my head as well.

I knew that I wanted to stand at the "crossroads" of the farm for the ceremony—the patch of sloping lawn between the front and the side of the house, the small spot of grass that links the orchard, the meadow, and the path that leads to the copse of old pines. Beyond the pines, the wide lawn that heads to the creek. The ramshackle springhouse that scared me so much stands at the lowest point of this patch, built over the natural spring that feeds our pond. Ungodly amounts of intestine-like tubes of tadpole eggs appear each spring, an astounding harbinger of life. Of rebirth.

The crossroads-lawn is a mere few steps from the house, so I knew I could be barefoot. I would feel the grass underneath my feet—the blades that I would tamp down with my footsteps—but they would stand again. They would feel the sun's rays, and they would grow. I wanted to be in touch with the ground, with the earth, when I married. I wanted to be tied to the world, to connect with the nature of the things—with my feet touching the grass that is rooted in the dirt that is the top layer of the earth that is part of a universe, I told her.

Lula reaches over and squeezes my arm.

It feels so real.

I am twenty-six years old. It's right here. It's today.

I am getting married. It's my wedding day. I will marry Eddie, my Eddie.

I look at myself one final time in the little mirror on the kitchen wall. I grab the orange and white and purple and yellow bouquet of flowers that Eddie picked first thing this morning. He surprised me, tickling my cheek with the tallest stalk of the Queen Anne's lace while I still slept. When I opened my eyes, he handed me a cup of coffee in my favorite crazy, chipped mug. I ran to the kitchen and put the wildflowers in an old mason jar filled with water and ice to keep them fresh.

I look down at my bare toes. This is so much like I always pictured it. How did I get this lucky? How did I find a man to love, to love me back? A man who not only fell in love with me, but with my childhood wish to be married at my family's farm? Who got a tear in his eye when I told it to him. Who kissed my hand and said: How could I not want to honor this dream of yours?

Eddie, my Eddie. I step across the threshold between the kitchen and the porch, and I get my first glimpse of you waiting to marry me. Our families are scattered about the lawn. I hear low voices, laughter. Your brother clears his throat and coughs into his hand. My brother pats him on the back.

As if you can sense my presence, you turn your head. You see me.

In one more second, I will step off the porch, and I will feel the grass underneath my feet and I will say the words and you will say the words and our eyes will stay locked to one another's and we will be a woman and a man who are united. With our families and the universe watching, we will be united.

I take a deep breath. One last look at the scene before I am in the middle of it. Woo picks up his violin and starts to play. It's time.

I swear I see movement at the edge of the orchard. Moving *away* from the gathering. Like someone was here and decided to leave, but who in the world would do that? No one, that's who. I must be more of an anxious bride than I thought. The old scaredy-cat me rearing her ugly little head. Wait; is that *fringe* I'm seeing? Long fringe, fluttering every which way? I know that fringe.

But Woo is playing. And I am imaging things. It's time.

I step off the porch.

When I step off the porch, I am lying in bed. It is the first time I have ever slept in the big bed—my aunt's bed. I have been lying awake for a long time.

We climbed the stairs hand in hand after everyone left: Woo and my parents and the little cousins grown tall and round but no less like fairies to me than always. We wanted this night, our first night as married lovers, all to ourselves. I lie here like a child on Christmas Eve, wanting to fall asleep so the morning will come faster. And being completely unable to fall asleep because I am too excited. I listen for your first light snores. I listen for them every night, as you always fall asleep before I do. Even when you tell me in the morning that you tossed and turned for countless time before you could fall asleep, I know better. I hear the snores. They thrill me. They comfort me. They make me feel like I am safe, like I am trusted.

You shift your head and nuzzle into your pillow. You clear your throat. One half of one snore escapes your mouth, and your eyes open wide as you say, Oh my God, a whip-poor-will!

I laugh out loud. You are a collector of birdsongs. I am used to this. You stubbornly remain in bed each morning until you hear at least one good, clear, unusual birdsong. Not "trash birds" as you refer to the rowdy collection of sparrows, starlings, wrens, and even robins that inhabit western Pennsylvania. Many a morning have I opened my eyes to you saying, Not a damn thing but trash birds this morning. I'm staying put until something better comes along. Even a cardinal. Might even settle for a mourning dove.

Did you hear it? you ask me. I mean, it could be a mockingbird. Could always be a mockingbird who's imitating a whippoor-will, but I'm counting it as a whip-poor-will.

I laugh again and trace my finger down the center of your face. A fire comes into your eye. You reach your hand around the back of my head and you pull me to you. We make love, again. Not like the first time tonight, not while we were still at the top of the stairs, tearing at each other's clothes, dropping to our knees on the raw oak floor.

We take our time. Even in the dark of the country night, we see one another. Our bodies are not nearly as naked as we are, in so many ways, on the night of our wedding.

I am the luckiest person in the world.

I savor that feeling—of my luck and my gratitude and my joy—as I sit with you on the porch swing. I am barefoot. My absolute favorite thing. I reach down with one toe, just my big toe, to give us the barest little push to keep the swing going. I feel tiny grains of dirt on the porch floor as my toe kisses against them. The extra length of the swing's chain clanks against the chain that supports the swing, hanging taut from the porch ceiling. How long has this swing been here? We have never once had to fix it or adjust it or anything. Not like the old wooden swing outside, with its absurdly long ropes hanging from the giant pine. We have had to fix that swing a million times it seems, but the porch one, never. I toss my head back and look up at the ceiling bolt that holds the swing in place, ancient and painted over so many times, the barest hints of pale orange rust leaking through the pigment. The thought of its strength, its endurance, amaze me. And makes me tired, exhausted. The strain of years upon years of holding up the weight of human beings. I twirl the extra chain through my fingers; I clunk it against the taut chain that is doing the work of holding us up. I look over at you. My Eddie. And now, my husband Eddie.

A line of sweat is just beginning to break out in the crease of your neck. I want to capture the expression on your face and put it in a jar. I want to carry the jar around with me like precious fireflies from a summer night. I have never seen you so relaxed, so contented. As if you know what I'm thinking, you reach for my hand and you kiss it. I am staring at you and you know that I am staring at you, and I tear up and you laugh. You kiss my hand again. You have that shy-but-formidable look, the one you had on our first date, our real first date. The look that makes your one dimple sing out. The look that made me think that maybe, just maybe, we might end up right here someday, swinging on this swing.

Your hand in mine is sweaty. The cool moistness of your palm against mine sends a ripple through my body, a shudder of feeling. I reach across your body to trace the line of sweat on your neck with the index finger of my other hand. I taste it. The salt of you. I cannot get enough of you.

You lean your head toward mine. You are going to kiss me. How many times have you kissed me, and my stomach still does a little leap? Your head jerks. What was that? you say. What was what, I say. I didn't hear anything. I definitely heard something, you say. You didn't hear that? Sounds like someone is throwing something—balls or something like that—one after another. Listen, you say. I hear it. Sounds like it's getting closer, you say. Sounds like it's coming from the orchard. You hear it, right? you ask me. Yes, I hear it.

Stay here. I'll check it out, you say. Probably some kid having a little fun, you say.

Don't be silly. I'll come, too, I say.

The short step down from the porch, my bare foot on the hot summer grass, I am hit by a wall of humidity. The full, fertile feel of the air that marks a Pennsylvania mountain summer. Thick, wet, ripe with a steaming, green life. "I love you as certain dark things are to be loved, in secret, between the shadow and the soul." That poem, the Pablo Neruda poem that you recited. The humidity reminds me. Down on one knee in an old-fashioned gesture I never would have guessed. Holding my hand and you said, "I love you as the plant that never blooms but carries in itself the light of hidden flowers." The wall of humidity pushes against me. Your arm reaches out and you tell me to stay back. Please, you say. Please stay back. "Thanks to your love a certain solid fragrance, risen from the earth, lives darkly in my body."

I see him, you say.

Then I see him, too.

I wonder what in the world he is doing here.

Without thinking I start to call out to him. I want to laugh. I want to wave and ask him what in the world he is doing here.

Then I see his face. "Lives darkly in his body."

And I know what he is doing here. I know.

I remember Ilsa and the bunny.

Sean has come to claim me.

I crouch down at the creek's edge and plunge my hands into the cool water. I spread my fingers wide, letting the creek's slow current flow over and around and between them. I turn my hands palms-side-up, raise them out of the creek, and watch the water run between my fingers.

Lula comes up behind me. She rests her hand on my shoulder to lower herself to the ground and sits beside me. Neither one of us says a word for a long, long time.

"Is Eddie all right, Lula?" I ask the same question a second time: "Is he all right?"

"He's not here, dear," Lula says.

"I'm not sure what I'm supposed to think," I say. "About that answer or about anything else." I can feel a single, silent tear making its way down my cheek. "Not sure at all." I keep saying the same things twice.

"When you told me what this place meant to you," Lula says, "—your treasured old family farm—you told me it was the place where there wasn't any 'supposed to.' There was just 'be.' "

"So, this is where my own words come back to haunt me?" I say. I am calm right now. My voice sounds reasoned, like I am asking a completely neutral question. "Gosh, I thought that didn't happen until you had children. I thought your kids were the ones who tossed your own words back at you."

"I suppose that's how it usually works," Lula says.

"But I didn't have children, did I, Lula?"

Lula says nothing.

"Sean killed me." I search Lula's face. She says nothing.

"It's all right; I figured it out. I died in the orchard. Sean killed me." I pause and think. "Which means that I'm dead, I think," I say. "I think that I must be dead."

"You're not dead, Mazie," Lula says.

"No? What, then?"

"In-between. You're in the space between life and no existence," Lula says.

"In-between." There is no expression in my voice, nor is

there any particular thought in my head. I am blank. Purely and utterly blank.

"Yes."

"In-between, but not dead," I say, again.

"Yes."

"Are you in-between, Lula?"

"No," Lula answers.

"Are you dead?"

"No," she says.

"Not dead or in-between." I think for a moment. "Are you alive? Are you a real person—a human being—who can see me?"

"No, Mazie. You can stop guessing. I'm something else entirely," she says. "I'm not trying to be vague, dear; it's difficult to explain. Sometimes I am a guide. Mostly, I am a witness. Always, I am a companion. For you. I am here for you."

"And why am I here?" I ask. "Does everyone stop off at their own in-between?"

"Very few people are in-between. Very few. There has to be a reason that you're here. There is something still to be done, or understood, about your life. Something essential. I have no idea what that might be."

"Oh, for God's sake, a million movie scenes come to mind here. Are you sure we're not stuck inside a movie? Is Clarence going to tell me that every time a bell rings an angel gets his wings, or Glenda will tell me to tap my heels together three times tap tap tap because the power has always been inside me, or...or is Norma Desmond ready for her close-up? Jesus Christ, Lula."

140

"You're shouting, dear," Lula says.

"Shouting? I'm shouting? I actually think I'm taking this whole thing rather well, Lula, this whole being dead thing."

"Not dead," Lula says.

"Sorry! My mistake! In-between!" My heavy breathing turns into gasping, hiccupping, and then into racking sobs. "This is not fair, Lula. Not fair."

"No, my darling girl," Lula says. "This is not fair at all."

Lula digs at the sandy soil along the creek's edge. She draws little patterns. I do nothing, nothing at all.

"I was with you at this creek once before," Lula says to me. "Do you remember?"

"Do you mean when I got soaked the other day? When I jumped in to see the salamander?"

"Yes, and the other part as well," she says simply.

"The other part? You mean when I relived the fragment where I ran into the creek barefoot? In the snow? After Sean... tried to kill himself?" I ask her.

"Yes, I mean that, too," Lula says.

"You mean you were here when I relived it or when it happened the first time, when I was fourteen?" I ask her.

Lula looks genuinely confused. "They're not different," she says. "Not distinct, different times."

I am exasperated, exhausted. I'm sad, too. Quite sad. It would feel so good to give up entirely. "I won't be asking any more questions just now."

...12

I sit with Eddie on the porch. Just now. Also just now, I watch the creek water drip through my fingers while, in the middle of the orchard, life drains from my body.

I am not ready to leave Eddie.

"Lula," I say, "I want to tell you something. I want to tell you about the first time Eddie and I went on a trip together. We went to Rocky Mountain National Park. We'd only been dating a couple of months. Eddie planned it. The whole thing. He wanted to make me happy, and he knew that being outside and hiking and immersed in the mountains would be perfect.

He found a little inn—equal parts cute and kitsch—with a remote-control fireplace in the room and our own Jacuzzi on the private outdoor deck. We arrived at night, popped open the bottle of wine Eddie had arranged to be waiting for us in the room. We couldn't stop playing with the remote, turning the fireplace on and off, laughing so hard we spilled red wine all over our clothes, so we ripped them off and ran naked out to the hot tub. That was when I learned that Eddie had a thing about water. Hot tub, shower, ocean—whatever—something took hold of him the second he got wet. He had an immediate and overpowering need to make love. So we did. In our own little hot tub on our own little deck of the room in Estes Park.

"The next morning was one of those Colorado days you remember your whole life. The sky so vast and blue that the whole world seems to be in sharper focus. We took an amazing hike—straight up, like pretty much all hikes in the mountains —and when we got to the topmost point, we kicked off our shoes and waded in a stream not so much bigger than this one. I took a picture of Eddie standing in the middle of that creek, right about the time he was saying to me, 'This may be the purest water we ever taste in our entire lives, baby. Drink up before we head down.'

"In a heartbeat, that blue sky darkened to a menacing, steely gray. The temperature dropped twenty degrees, and hail the size of marbles slammed us with such force it seemed like it must have the conscious intention of hurting us. We started running as fast as we could, and since it was a steep downhill and we were already lightheaded from the altitude, we felt like we must be flying. Flying and freezing and getting pelted by marbles. And laughing. Out of breath and exhausted as we were. Laughing so hard.

"Right about the time we could spot our car in the parking lot at the trail head, the hail stopped and the skies cleared. The temperature started to rise. Poof. The same stunningly beautiful, warm day as before. Like the universe just wanted to play a funny little trick on us. Know what else? That 'purest water we'll ever taste in our entire lives?' I got a parasite from drinking it. Was sick as a dog for months. That is, I believe, an outstanding example of the concept of irony. Eddie was fine, by the way. Pure, amazing luck that his particular mouthful of water did not have a single parasite, and mine did."

"Did you see Sean again, dear? After that period in high school?"

"I don't want to talk about Sean, Lula. I want to talk about Eddie." I look deep into Lula's eyes. I let the tears stream from my own. "He was right here. *Right here.* I want him back."

I crouch at the creek's edge and submerge both my hands in the cool water. I spread my fingers wide, letting the creek's slow current flow over and around and between them. I turn my hands palms-side-up, raise them out of the creek, and let the water run between my fingers.

With a great effort, Lula kneels beside me.

Neither of us says a word for quite a while.

"Yes, to answer your question. About Sean. There were three more 'Sean sightings'—as I thought of them. Three different times in my life. The first was my freshman year of college. I went to college too far away from home to come back for Thanksgiving. Christmas break marked the first time I had been home in four months.

"My own home felt strange and foreign. I had grown used to the sound that the springs of my cheap dorm bed made every time I moved a muscle in my cave-like lower bunk. My bedroom at home was larger than the one that two of us shared at school. But I didn't feel like I was in a comfortable and familiar place; my old room felt empty and hollow and filled with an awful void. I lay on my bed, staring up at my owl mobile just as I had spent countless hours through all of high school, trying to regain a sense of my home. The doorbell rang. I jumped up and ran to the stairs, eager to see who might be stopping by on Christmas Eve.

"A déjà vu of biblical proportions seized me. I called out to my mother, who came from the kitchen—wiping her wet hands on her apron and shooting me a this-had-better-be-good look. But one glance at me and her expression softened. She looked through the little glass pane of our front door. Sean stood there.

"My mother looked at me in a way I couldn't make any sense of, then she opened the door.

"I was still in high school when Sean dropped out—about a year after we broke up. Rumors abounded that he was living on the streets and had gotten involved in all kinds of crazy stuff. Only one guy from his old circle of friends had seen him, so I didn't give much credence to the tales and legends that occasionally floated around school.

"Like there was nothing the least bit complicated about it, my mother opened the door.

" 'Well, hello, Sean,' my mother said.

" 'Merry Christmas, Mrs. Mills,' Sean said. 'I brought these for the family.' He held out a brown grocery bag. My mother reached inside and pulled out a large plastic bag completely filled with kumquats.

" 'Kumquats, are they?' She had that singsongy voice I remembered from when Sean used to hang around. After he tried to kill himself.

" 'Kumquats, Mrs. Mills,' he said.

"If Sean hadn't been wearing the same buckskin jacket, the one with the crazy long fringe that was seared into my memory from the infamous night of the glistening razor and raging snowstorm, I'm not sure I would have recognized him. His raven black hair fell well past his shoulders in curls that might have been beautifully impressive if there was any evidence that he had washed or combed them in recent history. Even with bulky winter clothing underneath the buckskin jacket, I could see that his once-lean, tall body had wizened away to skeletal thinness. His formerly piercing blue blue eyes were sunken deep into his face, underlined by circles so thick and purple and horrific that he looked like someone may well have beaten the shit out of him. And those eyes, Sean's eyes, were no longer piercing. There was no longer a hint of his previous twinkle. His eyes were dead, as if there was nothing there at all. As if they no longer saw a thing.

"'Well, thank you so much,' my mother said. 'I'll go put them in the kitchen.'

"My mother turned on her heels. She walked away. She walked into the kitchen. And she stayed there. She left me alone with him.

"Sean reached to close the front door behind him, and with the movement of his arm, I got a whiff I could not believe. He smelled. Really, *really* bad. I was going to college in the inner city and had seen plenty of homeless people and drunks and junkies; I knew the smell.

"I wanted to slam the door in his sunken-eyed face. I wanted to scoop him up in my arms. I wanted to slap him. I wanted to save him. I wanted—more than anything—that Sean O'Connor had never rung our doorbell on Christmas Eve.

"We stood in the front doorway. Neither one of us moved. He gave me a plaintive smile.

"I had no idea what to say. I went with, 'Kumquats?'

"'I wanted to get something for your family. I went into the grocery store, and…I didn't know what to get. There was this mountain of them. Orange and beautiful, with their stems and their little green leaves still on…I don't know.' He snickered and reached out his arms to shrug. When he did, the overpowering smell again.

"'Sean, what the fuck?' I said. 'What in the world is going on? You look like shit.'

"'Well, you look beautiful,' he said.

"My mother called out from the kitchen, 'Woo and Dr. Mills

147

should be back from shopping any minute, Sean. Want some hot chocolate and cookies?'

"I was utterly, completely, mind-blowingly stunned that my mother had just invited Sean to stay longer. Tears welled in my eyes, and Sean saw them.

" 'Been living on the streets, but I'm gonna turn things around. I will. I promise. I'm not hooked. I swear. I do all different stuff, so I don't get hooked on any one thing. I'm smart about it. Admit I'm kind of a needle junkie, though. Totally addicted to shooting stuff—did you ever see anyone shoot up, Mazie? It's beautiful. Purely and utterly beautiful, watching the liquid and your own blood mix and swirl and go back and forth.'

"Tears streamed down my cheeks when he said this. My nose filled with snot, and I rubbed at it with my hand.

" 'I'm gonna turn it around, Mazie. You'll see.'

"Sean opened the door again, stepped outside, and was gone.

"The second Sean Sighting was my third year of college. I was living in a house with a bunch of people when one of my roommates handed me a letter that had been in the day's mail. It was written on pale blue, official-looking stationary. I recognized Sean's faint, whorled handwriting immediately, but did a double take when I saw the insignia for the United States Navy.

"Sean's letter said that he was stationed in San Diego. He wanted me to know that he had turned his life around completely. He was living a 'Navy life' and 'learning valuable skills for the future' and 'sticking strictly to the straight and narrow.'

148

It was a long, newsy, conversational letter. I knew what the punch line was going to be way before I got to it—he had never wavered from his belief that he and I belonged together, forever. And when he had served his time and proven himself and regained my trust, he would come for me.

"Sean sent regular letters the whole time he was in the Navy. I only answered once, to tell him that I wished him all the best in the whole world, but that a life with me was not in the cards.

"And finally, the third Sean Sighting.

"I don't know how he found out that I had met Eddie and that Eddie and I were serious. I don't know how he found out that I was visiting my parents. But somehow, he had learned both of those things. Again again again, he stood at my parents' front door, wearing his Navy peacoat. I said 'Sean,' but did not move aside to let him in. His eyes were alive again, but not like they had been before—when they had melted my thirteen-year-old soul. Not alive with life, but something else. He held up one hand. His index finger stopped at the second knuckle. The tip was gone, a cicatrix of scarred-over, torn skin still angry and red.

" 'I would do anything for you,' he said. He reached into his coat pocket and pulled out a baby food jar. The chopped-off tip of his finger bobbed around inside. I gasped, then screamed. I slammed the door in his face and never saw him again.

"Well. At least I never saw him again until. Until...I'm not really sure how to refer to time, Lula. Until that time when he killed me."

... 13

"I saw a movie once where there was a *Handbook for the Recently Deceased*. Something like that could come in mighty handy right about now."

"No handbook, I'm afraid," Lula says.

"So how does this work? Seriously. You say that I'm here for some reason. Something I'm supposed to figure out. How do I figure something out when I don't even know what the 'something' is?" There is another long silence before I ask Lula, "Am I going to have all my questions answered? When I leave the orchard? Everything I've ever wondered?"

"No," she says, "I'm afraid it doesn't work that way."

"Well, that sucks," I say. "Is that because you don't know the answers, or you won't tell? I don't mean 'you' as in Lula, I mean 'you' as in…whoever or whatever has the answers."

Lula sighs and folds her hands in her lap.

"Never mind," I say. "You know, so far I'd have to say that this whole entire in-between thing pretty much STINKS. I get the privilege of coming here for some reason that is completely unknown, and it's my mission to figure it out. But first I have to figure out how to figure it out. But it's in-between, meaning that at some point, I will have to leave."

"I suppose it's understandable that you would be peevish," Lula says.

And I can't help myself; I laugh out loud.

"Peevish," I say, "I don't believe I've ever heard anyone say that word aloud."

Lula moves her folded hands to the ground and runs her fingers through the moist dirt at the creek's edge. I pick up a smooth little stone and roll it between my thumb and index finger.

"Do I have a time limit, Lula?" I ask. "Are you going to kick me out one of these mornings? Tell me that it's time to move on?"

"No, Mazie. I'm not," she says. "You are free to stay as long as you like."

My voice catches in my throat. "And you, Lula? Are you free to stay for as long as you want? Will you get called back to…"

"I will not leave you, Mazie. Not unless you want me to go. If you want some time here by yourself."

"What if I don't want to leave? Ever."

151

"When the time is right, you'll be ready," Lula says to me.

"What if I'm never ready? I never wanted to leave, even when I was little. When Sunday evening came and it was time to leave the farm, my parents wanted to drag out the weekend as long as they possibly could. We all did. We'd sit around the supper table, everyone getting quieter and quieter. The cicadas' drone would swell and then fall as the sunlight faded. The lights of fireflies would appear here and there, sporadic, few and far between. We'd pack our stuff into the van, each of us knowing our tasks. By the time we were ready to hit the road, we would be immersed in that blacker-than-black of night in the woods." I feel it now. The end-of-the-weekend languor, the sadness at leaving. It's a confusing feeling, like I am partly gone from the place I'm still in. One foot already out…one still in.

"Do you know what my father used to do? Once we had packed everything up and piled into the car, he would drive out to the paved road and stop at the very topmost part of the mountain. My father would put the car in neutral, and he'd see if he could coast the entire way down, going faster and faster and faster, without once hitting the brakes. Around all those curves and bends. It seemed like total darkness to me—you know there aren't any streetlights out here. But sometimes, he'd turn the headlights off. He swore he could get a better look at the road without those pesky headlights. My brother Woo and I would yell, 'Weeeeeeeee, weeeeeeeeeee,' and we'd hold our feet up in the air—somehow that was part of the magic: our feet had to be held high up and never touch the floor of the car.

152

When we got to the bottom, we'd clap our hands and bounce up and down on the car seats and whoop it up like crazy."

Lula stares at me and says nothing. I have learned that this always masks something deeper, something she is thinking but doesn't want to say. "What?" I ask her.

Lula shifts uncomfortably in her chair. "Was that fun, Mazie?"

"Well, sure. I just said how my brother and I would be beside ourselves."

Lula looks straight ahead again for a moment and then says, "I'd certainly be beside myself. I'd be scared half to death."

It's my turn to look straight ahead. "You're a party pooper," I say. "Ever heard that expression? Know what it means?"

"Of course, I know what it means," Lula says. "Even if I hadn't heard it before, the expression is rather incontrovertibly self-evident. Do you know what that means? Incontrovertibly?"

"Why are you getting so cranky about this? I thought I was telling you about a fun adventure we had, and next thing I know you've gone all Smokey-the-Bear serious."

We are both silent for a long while, which makes me feel sad and helpless. But I'm also annoyed. Angry, even. Unreasonably so. My own sign that something lurks beneath my surface. "Did that honestly sound scary to you?"

"Yes," Lula says simply.

Again, we sit in silence.

"My father drank a lot."

"Yes, I remember you mentioned."

I swallow hard. "He started at eleven. Drinking, I mean. He checked his watch."

153

Lula says nothing.

"As if checking his watch and waiting until eleven o'clock made it better somehow."

Lula swishes a fly from her face. I squish a mosquito on my thigh. The mosquito makes an ungodly mess of bug pulp mixed with smears of my own blood. I lick my thumb and rub at the spot. "It seemed like we passed so many car accidents on those drives back home. Flashing lights and total chaos. People wandering through scenes of crushed vehicles and strewn wreckage. Every once in a while, we'd catch sight of someone lying on the ground. We'd all look as we drove by, and all four of us would give our assessment of whether we thought anyone had died. Sometimes, we were in complete agreement. It was easy to see that someone had. Inside of myself, I knew that could be us. My family. It could so easily have been us. I wondered which of us might live. Which of us would die."

A loud sigh escapes from me, unforeseen. My hands seem to be trembling. "We were in an accident, actually. My father lost control of the car somehow, and we careened all over the road, bouncing off the guardrail and across all the lanes. The world spun in circles through the windshield seemingly forever. We finally stopped when the third tire came off. The car was totaled. If another family had been driving past and assessed the accident like my own family did, they would have been certain we had all been killed. My mother broke her collarbone. The skin on my knee was completely scraped off, but I was fine otherwise. My father didn't have a scratch on him. Woo, in the back seat with me, hit his head, lost consciousness, and fell off the seat. When the first passerby stopped, he looked in and saw Woo on the floor of the car. Woo woke up just then, saw the stranger looking down on him, and said, 'Are you St. Peter?' My family laughed about that for years. Like it was the funniest thing in the world. 'Are you St. Peter?'"

Lula and I sit so long that the bright white light of the midday gets heavy with gold. Long enough that the gold loses its weight; its intensity fades and tinges of orange and a deeper, duller blue mix in and surround us. Long enough that the crickets and cicadas begin their late afternoon serenade.

Lula puts her hand around the round of my shoulder and kneads it. Neither of us has spoken a word for a very long while when I say, "Of course I was scared." I'm not even sure if I've spoken or if the words are still in my mind when I can feel it.

I am in the car. Our old VW van—with the middle seat removed. My parents are a million miles away in their separate front seats. It is so totally dark that I can't actually see them; I have to imagine that they are there. We are coasting down the mountain. How can my father see a single thing? I strain my eyes, but I get no sense of the road. The tires squeal, and a curve throws me against the side of the car. They squeal again and I crash against Woo. I am going to pee in my pants, I'm sure of it. My heart is beating so fast, racing, thumping against my ribs; it's going to rip right through my chest and I am concentrating so so hard on yelling, Weeeeeeeeeeeee, as loud as I can because it tells me I am still here I am still alive as long as I can hear the sound of my own voice, I am still here. And I am so ashamed, so ashamed of how scared I am.

Tears stream down my face and I say to myself, *No, you can't cry. You can't! You aren't allowed to cry.* But that just makes me cry harder. I am sobbing, and I can't stop no matter how much I try to turn my screaming sobs back into shouting, Weeeeeeeeeeeeee.

Lula cups her hand against my cheek.

And it's all gone.

The first firefly of the evening lights up under the farthest of the tall pines.

Lula takes her hand away.

Oh my God. Oh, my GOD! I can't believe it! I cannot believe it's taken me this long to figure it out. I can't believe it! "It's when you touch me," I say to her. "Something happens when you touch me. That's it, isn't it? You make me go somewhere. And then later, you bring me back. *You* make it all happen! When you touch me!"

"I open a door. That's all I do," she says.

"You're in control of all this! You've always been in control of all this!" I am outraged, indignant. I have no idea why. I feel like I am a pawn even in my own death. I want to punch her in the face. I want to see if she will bleed, if she has blood that will spill just like mine did. I want to see it.

"You're the one 'in control,' to use your expression," she says to me. "I just open the door. You are the one who chooses where to go," Lula says. "You're the one who chose to come to the farm in the first place."

"I did? I figured I ended up here because it's where I died. Was murdered, I should say. Maybe it will help if I say the

156

whole thing out loud: I, Mazie, was murdered by Sean under an apple tree in the orchard of my old family farm." I wait for a few seconds. "Nope. Nothing. No magic by saying it."

"The point is you make all the choices. All I do is touch you. Everything that happens after that is chosen by you."

"What am I choosing? I don't understand! I don't understand any of this. For all I know, I'm actually in some hospital room right now, on life support, and every single bit of this, every one of these…encounters…that I have had with you, are a flash through my brain, a comforting and peaceful explanation that my own mind has manufactured, a little zap at the very second that I take my final breath. I've read about things like that. Truly, Lula, that would make more sense than believing any of this is…'real.' My loving family could be huddled around my bed right now, sobbing their eyes out, steeling themselves, and gathering their courage to pull the plug."

"What do you mean real?" Lula's voice is strangely low, quiet.

"You know, REAL, as in, it actually exists."

"How could everything, how could *anything*, not be real?" she asks.

"You understand that if *you* aren't real in the first place, Lula, this whole discussion pretty quickly becomes circular."

"Do you not feel the wind when it blows on your face, Mazie? The warmth of the sun's midday rays? I see you turn your face toward the sun so often. When you go barefoot, do you not feel each different thing that is under your feet: the damp morning grass, the painted wood of the porch floor, the worn ridges of the paving stones?"

I look Lula up and down. I consider what she is saying, though I don't know *how* to consider it yet.

"When you plunged into the creek, did the rocks on the bottom scrape against your knees? Did the water run between each of your fingers when you lifted them out of that same creek; did you feel the slippery weight of it? The coolness? The day that you were telling me about your great-aunt Lula and you inadvertently sniffed me: did you smell my smell? My completely unique Lula smell?" She sniffs. "You *did,* Mazie. I know that you did." She seems like her feelings are hurt. Like I am *not getting it,* and the fact that I'm not getting it is wounding her. She waits for a moment, then adds, "You are completely yourself here, just the same as you were in your life. Just the same. I've been with you; I've watched you; I've seen you. You notice *everything.* Everything."

I'm not really sure what she means by that, probably because my mind is elsewhere. "Hold it," I say. "I have a question. About me being the one 'in charge.' You said that I'm the one who chose to come back to my old family farm. I wasn't compelled to return here because I died here. I chose it. But what about after I came here? Does everyone in-between relive parts of their life in order to understand something? The vital thing they need to figure out?"

"No, everyone has his or her own individual path," she says.

"So, *I'm* the one who's choosing to relive things? Me?"

"Exactly so."

I think for a long time. The longer I think, the less I am sure about anything at all.

"Was there an Eddie, Lula? Did Sean murder me when I was fourteen?"

Lula says nothing.

"Maybe I should ask if there was really even a Sean. Maybe I fell off the edge of the Grand Canyon when I was four years old."

Lula smiles. A gentle, patient smile.

"I wish I had gotten more time, Lula."

...14

I have remembered so much. So many moments, entire days as well. Some of them perfectly ordinary —the way the wind moved through the field on a particular morning. The bloom of a lone trillium bursting through the winter decay of the forest floor. The unique creaks and moans of the porch swing, the twin beds, the screen door, the spring on the outhouse door—each of them timeless, unchanged from the day my family arrived here. Each of them emblazoned within me. Some of the memories have been of extraordinary things—my little cousins dancing and shrieking and holding hands during their first thunderstorm, the earth quivering under my feet from the power of the thunder.

Eddie turning his face from side to side, his mouth dropping open, the joy that gushed from him as we drove down the road to the farm the first time.

But these are memories, treasures that live inside of me. They are close. I reach out and I touch them and I show them to Lula. The hidden things are different. They are not memories that I recall, but, rather, parts of my life that I *relive*. The hidden things are not inside of me. When they descend, I am inside of them.

There is a poem by Rainer Maria Rilke:

> Ignorant before the heavens of my life,
> I stand and gaze in wonder. Oh the vastness
> of the stars. Their rising and descent. How still.
> As if I didn't exist. Do I have any
> share in this? Have I somehow dispensed with
> their pure effect? Does my blood's ebb and flow
> change with their changes? Let me put aside
> every desire, every relationship
> except this one, so that my heart grows used to
> its farthest spaces. Better that it live
> fully aware, in the terror of its stars, than
> as if protected, soothed by what is near.

What am I but "ignorant before the heavens of my life?" I travel within my own existence. I live certain things again, which would seem a great gift, if only I knew why.

The first time I journeyed back in my own life was when

Lula brought the jewelweed. She handed me the flowers, and with her touch I travelled. I lay on the ground in the orchard, head-to-head with Woo, staring at the clouds. The bristles of his buzz cut pressing into my scalp. Flyaway strands of my hair blowing across my cheeks. His timothy grass chaw waving back and forth. A seemingly simple afternoon. But I told Lula it had been one of the best days of my life, and it was.

The second time was when I told her why my parents had decided to buy the farm, after our one and only family vacation road trip. A wilderness of heat and dust and hours upon hours in the back seat. For just a moment, I was on my uncle's boat, the sea heaving and the scary baby cousin puking. It was the dream I had after that trip that I lived again. The scrape of my saddle shoe against the packed dirt at the edge of the Grand Canyon. The skin being scoured from my calf. A million stars shooting from my body as I died.

The third time. Diving into the creek after Sean tried to kill himself.

The fourth. The day of my wedding. Oh my God, my God, seeing Eddie, seeing him looking at me.

And the last time, the fifth time. Driving home. Coasting down the mountain in the black nothingness.

Coasting down the mountain in the black nothingness.

Terrifying. It was terrifying. I thought my eyeballs would explode out of my face from the panic. I felt it again, every bit of it. EVERY BIT OF IT. A little kid, a *really* little kid, getting into a car with a father who had been drinking all day long. A father who turned off the headlights on a mountain road and refused to put on the brakes until he was at the rock bottom of the mountain.

My God. Who does that? WHO DOES THAT? That's insane! How did my parents not know that was totally insane?

Lula is not here. She has not touched me. Nonetheless I am on the porch with her. It is just a short while after we have met. I drop into the middle of the exact conversation Lula and I had. I am telling her about our trip to California.

I am saying, "Days and days of endless barren landscapes, our spanking new station wagon throwing up a dust storm that followed in our wake. No air conditioning. The windows were wide open, making any kind of talking sort of impossible. It was dry and dusty, with a hot wind blowing in our faces all day long. My brother and I bounced and blew around in the back seat in a woozy stupor. Every so often, one of us would come out of our haze long enough to let out a plaintive whine of 'How much longer?' or, even more important, 'Are you sure there's a POOL?' "

"I was pretty sure my parents were tricksters," I say to Lula. I'm surprised to find myself saying this. It's a big thing to confess— what a weird and suspicious little kid I was. But it's true. From an early age, I was watching them out of the corners of my eyes.

Lula says, "Maybe you just noticed things."

That's all. After Lula says that line, I am out of the relived moment. I wander the length of the L-shaped porch. I smooth a corner of the blue embroidered coverlet that lies on the day-bed. I give the swing a gentle push and listen to the extra length of chain swoosh against the support chain. I open the screen door on my way past it and savor the sound of its slam. I run my hand along the Naugahyde seam of the chair that used to be my mother's. Finally, I ring the cow bell in the far corner of the porch, the one that told Woo and me it was time to come in from our adventures. It marked the end of the day.

"Maybe you just noticed things."

Is that possible?

Is it possible that I noticed things? Real things. The things that were going on inside of the people around me. Their dark places. Their chaos. Their bullying. Their obliviousness to the people *around them*. Is it possible that I was not the cowardly, nervous, eternally apprehensive child that I thought I was?

Is it possible that the people around me were scary!

> Better that it live
> fully aware, in the terror of its stars...

...15

A summer shower—so gentle that it makes no sound—begins. I strain my eyes to look through the screen, trying to focus on the mist-fine drops that are falling. I stand, which jars the porch swing into a crazy lopsided twist. The excess chain slaps its wonderful, clangy slap against the main chain. I laugh out loud at it. I press my nose against the screen, knowing it will leave a smudge, to get a better look at the silent rain.

I make no noise, walking slowly and carefully to the screen door, not wanting to add a single sound to the perfect, beautiful rain shower. I close the door carefully behind me, holding the latch hook with my thumb to make sure it doesn't clink against the door. I stand on the flagstone just outside the door, feeling the rain on the top of my head. I step off the stone so I can stand on the grass, so I can feel the blades covered with their tiny droplets of life-giving water.

The rain comes down a wee tad harder. I spread my arms wide and raise my face to the sky. I try to see if I can keep from blinking when the raindrops hit my closed eyes. I can't, and this makes me laugh. When I do, the raindrops hit my teeth. One finds its way into an opening and lands in my mouth. I taste its fresh-rain taste and let it spread across my tongue until it is a part of my saliva and, thereby, a part of me.

I can hear individual drops now. I hear especially fat ones when they plop onto a frond on one of the struggling ferns, when they land on the dark, waxy leaves of the mountain laurel. They stay where they land; the leaves hold them.

One good summer shower is all it takes for the world to come back to life. Tomorrow, like a miracle, green shoots will find their way through the tangled, dried, brown field. The grass of the lawn will look as it does at the swell of spring. I don't need to see it to know that it will happen. I know that it will happen because I have seen it, I did see it. Knowing that it will go on, that everything will go on, without me, gives me great comfort.

Lula was right. I did notice everything.

I have felt unfettered joy from moments as simple as Woo's buzz cut against my scalp as we lay in the rocky orchard to the unbounded euphoria of my wedding day.

I have known what it is like to be alone and terrified. A four-year-old, without anyone watching, teetering on the edge of the Grand Canyon. An eight-year-old in a car that flirted with death on its brakeless course down a mountain road. When things were scary, I was scared. When they were jaw-droppingly terrifying, I was terrified.

Sean. No one should have to try so hard to convince the people around them that they are in danger. Long before Sean brought me the cut-off tip of his finger inside a bottle of formaldehyde, I knew he had dark and hidden places. I knew he was dangerous. I saw it when no one else did.

> Better that it live
> fully aware, in the terror of its stars...

Whatever time I had, I *was* fully aware.

Awareness allowed me to love. I felt great, great love. Love that lifted me, that enabled me to know both myself and the world more deeply. Eddie. Lula.

I know why I am here, in-between.

I am here to understand this: I had a magnificent life.

After word

After
word

I'm ready.

Lula is next to me on the swing. I look down at my hands, resting on top of a thick blanket to fend off the morning chill. They no longer look like my hands. In the craggy blue veins, I see the branches of ancient, sturdy trees lifting to the sky. I see their deep, formidable roots, reaching down, down into the earth. I see water flowing through creeks and streams and rivers.

I am old.

I know that I did not grow old in real life. But I can't say that...I can't say "real life." Because this is what I know now: it is all real.

It is one final gift, to see my own hands, old like Lula's, as we sit together one last time.

"Lula," I say, "will you stay here? On the porch? On the swing? I'm thinking that…when I walk into the orchard…when I get to the spot…the spot where…that I'll go on. I'll no longer be in-between."

Lula says, "Yes, dear." She reaches for my hand and holds it tight. Nothing happens when she touches me now. Our work is done.

"I'd like to think of you as staying here. That you've always been here and always will be. I'd like to walk into the orchard with that thought."

"Of course, Mazie," Lula says to me.

I stand and take a look around the porch of our old family farm. I take the first few steps, and my breath catches in my chest. But as I step down onto the path, then onto the grass, the sun catches me directly on the side of my face.

Who knows, maybe I died a long, long time ago. Maybe I have not yet been born. Maybe, just maybe, both are true.

• • • • • • • • •

Acknowledgments

Two people consistently went above and beyond in their support of *The Rocky Orchard*—how amazing that both of them are also part of my publishing team at Amika Press. My editor John Manos had a strong feeling for this book when I shared the initial idea with him over a taco lunch. He believed in it well before I did, and his solid, unwavering belief was the bedrock that kept me afloat.

Sarah Koz made herself available to read anything and everything I was willing to send her, right from the beginning—which is completely outside of her work for the press. Sarah describes herself as a "mean" reader, which is exactly what I wanted—a deeply serious reader who would not hesitate to tell me whenever I veered off track, every step of the way. It turned out Sarah was not mean at all. She proved unwavering in her support and in her devotion to the book. When she made suggestions, I listened.

I am grateful to my early readers of rough drafts: Karen Monier, James Petersen and Janis Post.

Hearty thanks to my wonderful writers group members, who bore with me through my presentation of material that came into their hands out of sequence and in pieces—in a book that's especially difficult to grapple with when it's *in order*. Thank you Laura Allen-Simpson, Bill Horstman, and Brooke Laufer.

I know that my children will eventually read this book. I know that they will love it beyond reason, even if they don't happen to like it. I anticipate that they will be mighty pleased to find that their mother has written a work of fiction where not one character, nor one event, nor anything whatsoever seems strangely familiar.

Jonathan, thank you for listening to everything I read aloud to you moments after I have written it. It's that swoon-like response that lifts me, as if my words are so compelling that you have lost your balance. That has a mighty power.

Barbara Monier has been writing since her earliest days when she composed in crayon on paper with extremely wide lines. She studied writing at Yale University and the University of Michigan. While at Michigan, she received the Avery and Jule Hopwood Prize. It was the highest prize awarded that year and the first in Michigan's history for a piece written directly for the screen. *The Rocky Orchard* is the latest of her four novels. *Pushing the River* (Amika Press), *You, In Your Green Shirt* and *A Little Birdie Told Me* (available on Amazon) are her previous titles.

www.ingramcontent.com/pod-product-compliance
Lightning Source LLC
Chambersburg PA
CBHW010833250626
47157CB00010B/3272